kis
succumbing to the sensual spell that
made her feel as if she and the man
holding her to his heart were the last
two people on earth.

Griffin's heart slammed against his ribs when he showered kisses around Belinda's lips and along her jaw. Lowering his head, he fastened his mouth along the column of her velvety, scented neck, nipping, suckling, licking her as if she were a frothy confection.

"You taste and smell so good," he mumbled over and over.

Baring her throat, Belinda closed her eyes. She wanted to tell Griffin that he felt and smelled good but the words were locked in her throat when a longing she'd never known seized her mind and body, refusing to let her go.

Books by Rochelle Alers

Kimani Romance

Bittersweet Love

Silhouette Desire

A Younger Man
*The Long Hot Summer
*Very Private Duty
*Beyond Business

*The Blackstones of Virginia

ROCHELLE ALERS

has been hailed by readers and booksellers alike as one of today's most popular African-American authors of women's fiction. With nearly two million copies of her novels in print, Ms. Alers is a regular on the Waldenbooks, Borders and *Essence* bestseller lists, and has been the recipient of numerous awards, including the Gold Pen Award, the Emma Award, the Vivian Stephens Award for Excellence in Romance Writing, the *Romantic Times BOOKreviews* Career Achievement Award and the Zora Neale Hurston Literary Award. A native New Yorker, Ms. Alers currently lives on Long Island. Visit her Web site at www.rochellealers.com.

Bittersweet Love

ROCHELLE ALERS

NATIONAL BESTSELLING AUTHOR

KIMANI ™
ROMANCE

If you purchased this book without a cover you should be aware
that this book is stolen property. It was reported as "unsold and
destroyed" to the publisher, and neither the author nor the
publisher has received any payment for this "stripped book."

To Michele Robinson…
A true Philadelphia princess.

Hear, O children, a father's instruction,
be attentive, that you may gain understanding!

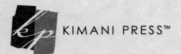

KIMANI PRESS™

Recycling programs
for this product may
not exist in your area.

ISBN-13: 978-0-373-86096-8
ISBN-10:   0-373-86096-X

BITTERSWEET LOVE

Copyright © 2009 by Rochelle Alers

All rights reserved. The reproduction, transmission or utilization
of this work in whole or in part in any form by any electronic, mechanical
or other means, now known or hereafter invented, including xerography,
photocopying and recording, or in any information storage or retrieval
system, is forbidden without written permission. For permission please
contact Kimani Press, Editorial Office, 233 Broadway, New York, NY
10279 U.S.A.

This is a work of fiction. Names, characters, places and incidents are
either the product of the author's imagination or are used fictitiously,
and any resemblance to actual persons, living or dead, business establishments,
events or locales is entirely coincidental.

® and TM are trademarks. Trademarks indicated with ® are registered in
the United States Patent and Trademark Office, the Canadian Trade Marks
Office and/or other countries.

www.kimanipress.com

Printed in U.S.A.

Dear Reader,

Belinda, Myles and Chandra Eaton come from a family of Pennsylvania teachers, but they are about to learn something about love they could never find in a textbook.

In *Bittersweet Love,* Philadelphia high-school history teacher Belinda Eaton has made it a practice to avoid Griffin Rice. Now she finds her future inexorably entwined with his when they share custody of their goddaughters following a family tragedy. In this story, Belinda encounters a very different Griffin when the high-profile sports attorney romances her, and proves he can be a loving father *and* husband.

In the second installment of THE EATONS trilogy, law professor Myles Eaton has never forgotten the woman who jilted him two weeks before their wedding to marry another man. But when he comes face-to-face with recently widowed Zabrina Cooper at his sister's wedding, he must decide whether to walk away or exact his own *Sweet Revenge.*

In *Sweet Dreams,* the final story of the Kimani Romance trilogy, elementary schoolteacher Chandra Eaton returns to Philadelphia after a two-year stint in the Peace Corps, and is distressed when she finds that she's misplaced the journals in which she recorded her highly erotic dreams. Her life changes dramatically when celebrated playwright Preston Tucker informs Chandra that he's found her journals. She is faced with the dilemma of walking away from the man she loves, because Preston's latest play is based on her journal entries.

But before you enjoy the next two EATONS books, look for the next story in the Hideaway series from Arabesque. The next Hideaway-saga book, *Secret Agenda* features Diego Cole-Thomas and Vivienne Neale, whose romance takes them from business to pleasure.

This summer, wedding bells will ring again, but this time it's the guys who fall in love in THE BEST MEN series from Arabesque. Three childhood friends are so focused on career success that they are reluctant to give up their carefree bachelorhood. Nevertheless, in one unforgettable year, each man will meet an extraordinary woman who will make him rethink love *and* marriage.

Yours in romance,

Rochelle Alers

Prologue

No one sitting in Grant and Donna Rice's family room had even noticed Belinda Eaton's brittle smile, clipped replies or that her delicate chin was set at a stubborn angle. They had come together to celebrate the birthday of twelve-year-old fraternal twins Sabrina and Layla Rice.

The two girls took turns opening envelopes, reading birthday cards, unwrapping gifts and hugging and kissing their parents as well as both sets of grandparents and their aunt and uncle.

Belinda, the twins' aunt, hadn't realized she was grinding her teeth until she felt the pain in her gums. It was either clench her jaw or spew expletives that were poised precipitously on the tip of her tongue. Her eyes narrowed when the object of her fury flashed his Cheshire cat grin.

That's it! she raged inwardly. *It ends tonight.* Brac-

ing her hands on the arms of the club chair, she rose to
her feet and made her way to where Griffin Rice stood
with his arm around his mother's shoulders. The expressive eyebrows that framed his olive-brown face arched
with her approach.

"Excuse me, Mrs. Rice, but I'd like to speak to your
son." Belinda deliberately neglected to acknowledge
Griffin by name.

Griffin Rice's large, deep-set dark brown eyes
widened appreciably. Whenever he saw his brother's
sister-in-law, which wasn't often enough, she looked
different. Belinda had a wealth of thick dark hair that
she'd styled in a ponytail. The soft glow from the
recessed lighting in the room flattered her flawless sable
face. A light dusting of makeup accentuated her exotic
slanted eyes, high cheekbones, short nose and gener-
ously curved lips.

A hint of a smile lifted the corners of his lips as he
stared boldly at the fullness of her breasts under a burnt-
orange cashmere pullover, which she'd paired with
black wool slacks and suede slip-ons. He'd always
found her alluring, but Belinda gave off a vibe that made
her seem snobbish and aloof. She'd been that way at
nineteen, and now at thirty-two she was even more
standoffish. Her request to speak to him was somewhat
shocking yet a pleasant surprise.

"Where would you like to talk?"

"Outside."

The response came across as a direct order and
Griffin curbed the urge to salute her. He pressed a kiss
to Gloria Rice's forehead. "I'll be right back, mother."
Grabbing Belinda's arm, he steered her toward the rear
of the house.

"The front porch," Belinda ordered again. The back porch was too close to the kitchen and she didn't want anyone to overhear what she had to say to him.

Reversing course, Griffin led her through the dining and living rooms and out to the front porch of the modest Dutch Colonial–style house. He held the front door open, waiting for Belinda to precede him, then stepped out onto the porch and closed the door behind them.

Leaning against a thick column on the porch, he slipped his hands into the pockets of his slacks and crossed his feet at the ankles. The seconds ticked off as Belinda sat on a cushioned love seat. Twin porch lanterns flanking the door provided enough light for him to make out her features. Griffin glanced away to look at the large autumnal wreath hanging on the door.

"What do you want to talk about?"

Belinda sat up, her spine ramrod straight. "What the hell do you think you're doing buying the girls a PlayStation when I told you that I planned to give it to them for Christmas?"

Nothing moved on Griffin, not even his eyes as he glared at the woman who was godmother and aunt to his nieces. "You told me nothing of the sort."

"When I spoke to Donna and asked what the girls wanted for their birthday she told me to give them gift cards for their favorite stores and to save the electronics for Christmas. I also remember her saying that she was going to tell you the same thing." She'd given her nieces gift cards to several popular clothing stores.

"Your sister didn't say anything to me, so take it up with her."

"No, Griffin, I'm taking it up with you. Every year you do this. We talk beforehand about what we're going to give the twins for Christmas and their birthdays, and invariably you do the complete opposite." She stood up and closed the distance between them. "This is the last time I'm going to let you play Big Willie to my nieces."

"*Your* nieces, Lindy?" he said mockingly. "How did you come to that conclusion when they're *my* brother and your sister's daughters?" He held up a hand when she opened her mouth to come back at him. "Unlike you, I don't have the time or the inclination to hang out in the mall. Layla and Sabrina said they wanted an Xbox, Wii or PlayStation, and I gave them the PlayStation."

Belinda closed her eyes rather than stare at Griffin Rice's gorgeous face. As an attorney for some of sports' biggest superstars, Griffin had become a celebrity in his own right. Paparazzi snapped pictures of him with his famous clients, glamorous models, beautiful actresses and recording stars. His masculine features, cleft chin and exquisitely tailored wardrobe afforded him a spot on the cover of *GQ*. He not only looked good, but he smelled delicious. His cologne was the perfect complement to his natural scent.

"Next time speak to me before you decide to give them what they want."

"Are you asking or telling me, Belinda?"

Her chest rose and fell, bringing his gaze to linger on her breasts. "I'm asking you, Griffin," she said in a softer tone.

Straightening, Griffin stared down at his sister-in-law, wondering if she was aware of how sexy she was. If he'd had a teacher who looked like Belinda Eaton he would've failed, just to have to repeat her class.

He dipped his head and brushed a kiss over her ear. "I'll think about it." Turning on his heels, Griffin went back into the house, leaving Belinda staring at his back as he walked away.

Her fingers curled into fists. She'd called him out for nothing. He had no intention of checking with her. It was as if they were warring parents competing to see who could win over their children with bigger and more expensive gifts.

She folded her arms under her breasts and shook her head. There was no doubt Griffin would continue to undermine her when it came to their nieces, but there was one thing she admired about the man: since he wasn't a father himself, he'd spared some woman a lifetime of grief.

Belinda waited on the porch a few minutes longer until the dropping temperature forced her indoors. Affecting a bright smile, she walked into the dining room in time to sing happy birthday before Sabrina and Layla blew out the candles and cut their cake.

Chapter 1

The soft-spoken attorney shook hands with Belinda Eaton and then repeated the gesture with Griffin Rice. "Congratulations, Mom, Dad. If you need a duplicate copy of the guardianship agreement I recommend you call this office rather than go to the Bureau of Records. I've heard that they always have a two-to-three-month backlog."

Belinda still could not believe she was to share parenting of her twin nieces with her sister's brother-in-law. Less than a year after she became an aunt, her sister had asked Belinda to raise her daughters if anything should happen to her and her husband. At that time she'd wondered, *why would a happily married, twenty-two-year-old woman with two beautiful children think about dying?* Apparently, her older sister, Donna, was more prophetic than she knew. Just weeks after the twins' twelfth birthday, their mother and father had been killed instantly when a drunk driver lost control of his pickup, crossed the median and collided head-on with their smaller sedan.

Belinda forced a smile. The meeting with the attorney and signing the documents that made her legal guardian of her twelve-year-old nieces had reopened a wound that was just beginning to heal. Her sister and brother-in-law had died days after Thanksgiving and it'd taken four months for their will to be probated.

"Thank you for everything, Mr. Connelly."

Impeccably dressed in a tailored suit, Jonathan Connelly stared at the young schoolteacher whose life was about to dramatically change. Her nieces were moving from the two-bedroom condo where they were temporarily living with their maternal grandparents into her modest house in a Philadelphia suburb. Although the children had been well cared for by their grandparents, Jonathan, the executor of her sister and brother-in-law's estate, felt that the emotional and social interests of the twin girls would be best served living with their aunt.

His shimmering green eyes lingered briefly on her rich nut-brown attractive face with its high cheekbones, slanting dark brown eyes and hair she wore in a flattering curly style. With her wool gabardine suit with a peplum jacket, pumps and the pearl studs that matched the single strand gracing her slender neck, Belinda appeared more like a young executive than a high school history teacher.

"If you need legal advice on anything, please don't hesitate to call me," Jonathan said, smiling.

A slight frown began to creep across Griffin Rice's good looks. "I believe I can help her with any legal problem," he said curtly. Griffin intended to make sure that he was available for Belinda if she needed legal counsel.

He had spent the better part of an hour watching Jonathan Connelly subtly flirt with his sister-in-law. He and Belinda shared guardianship of their nieces, but he'd be damned if he'd allow the smooth-talking, toothpaste-ad-smiling, little-too-slick-for-Griffin's-taste attorney take advantage of her.

Although they were related through marriage, Griffin and Belinda hadn't spent much time together and when they did, they usually butted heads. Most of the time, he was involved in contract negotiations for his pro-athlete clients or taking a much-needed vacation. And whenever he invited her to his home for an informal get-together, she always declined. The last time they had been together was when the two families were making funeral arrangements for Grant and Donna.

Reaching out, he cupped Belinda's elbow. "I think it's time we leave."

Belinda forced herself not to pull away from the pressure of Griffin's hand on her arm. She didn't like him, had never really liked him, but now they were thrown together because they shared custody of their nieces. She didn't know what her sister was thinking when she and Grant decided on Griffin as the girls' guardian. The high-profile, skirt-hopping sports attorney lacked the essentials for fatherhood.

She gave Jonathan a dazzling smile that curved her full, sensuous mouth. "If I need your assistance, I won't hesitate to call you."

Belinda sensed her brother-in-law's annoyance at her rebuff of his offer of legal help when his fingers tightened around her elbow. At five-six and one hundred thirty pounds she knew she was physically no match for Griffin's six-two, one hundred ninety pound viselike grip. Glancing over her shoulder, she glared at him.

"I'm ready."

Griffin led Belinda out of the lawyers' offices and waited until she was seated in his late-model Lexus hybrid and he was beside her before he allowed himself to draw a normal breath.

"Did I not say that I would take care of your legal concerns?"

Belinda shifted on the leather seat, glaring at the cleft in the chin of an otherwise incredibly handsome man who'd landed unceremoniously in her life. She'd lost count of the number of times women colleagues had asked her whether Griffin was available.

"Watch your tone, Griffin. I'm not one of your dim-witted girlfriends who is honored just to be in your presence." Belinda knew she'd struck a nerve when she saw his flushed face.

"In case you didn't notice, the man wasn't looking to offer legal advice."

She frowned. "Then please tell me what he was offering."

"His bed."

Griffin's comment caught her off guard for several seconds. "How would you know that?" Belinda said when she recovered her composure.

A subtle smile parted Griffin's lips as his gaze slipped from Belinda's face to her breasts and back to her stunned expression. "I'm a man, Belinda. And as such, I recognized all the signals Jonathan was sending your way."

Heat pricked little pinpoints across Belinda's skin as she struggled not to look away from the large dark eyes that were sending sensuous flames through her body.

She couldn't move or blink. "Not every man who looks at me wants me in *that* way, Griffin."

Griffin's smile widened. "With your face and your body, you look nothing like the spinster schoolmarm."

"Wrong century and definitely wrong woman," she countered. "I'm not a schoolmarm but an educator. And whether I'm thirty-two or sixty-two I'll never think of myself as a spinster."

"The fact remains that Jonathan wants you. So I suggest that you not lead him on *if* or *when* you need legal advice. And, the offer still holds. If you need a lawyer, then I'm always available to you."

She shook her head. "Why would I need you when my brother is a lawyer?" Her older brother, Myles, had recently resigned as partner at a leading Philadelphia law firm to teach at Duquesne, a private university law school in Pittsburgh.

Griffin inserted the keyless fob in the ignition slot and pushed a button, starting up the SUV. "Just make certain you use *him*."

As Griffin maneuvered out of the parking lot, Belinda wondered if he was as brusque with the women he dated or slept with. Other than his looks and his money, she didn't know why any of them would put up with his attitude.

They'd agreed that the girls would stay with her during the week and with Griffin on the weekends. But she doubted, with his busy social life, that there would be many weekends that the twins would stay with Griffin. That suited Belinda just fine, because what they needed more than anything was stability.

Sabrina and Layla Rice had lost both parents and since then had been living with their grandparents for the past four months. Now they would be moving again when they came to live with her. The fallout after the funeral and burial was difficult when grandparents and relatives began arguing about who would raise the twins. As an investment banker, Grant Rice and his family had been financially sound. And the prospect of the girls' inheritance drew relatives Griffin hadn't known or seen in decades like hungry sharks to the smell of blood.

The speculation as to the extent of Grant's wealth ended when Griffin announced that he and Belinda were the legal guardians, and that Belinda was the beneficiary of Grant and Donna's multimillion-dollar insurance policy. He had inherited vacant parcels of land that developers were interested in. The only thing he and Belinda had agreed upon was that all the proceeds and profits would be put aside for their nieces' education and financial future.

Belinda had used the few months that the girls were living with their grandparents to decorate her house to accommodate the growing twins. She wanted the transition to be smooth and stress-free for everyone involved. She'd had more than ten years of teaching young adults, but this was to be the first time Belinda would become a parent in every sense of the word.

The drive from downtown Philadelphia to a nearby suburb was accomplished in complete silence. When Griffin turned off into the subdivision and parked in the driveway where her parents had purchased the town house after selling the large house where they'd raised their four children, Belinda was out of the car before Griffin could shut off the engine. She didn't see his scowl, but registered the slam of the driver's-side door when he closed it.

Ringing the bell, she waited for her mother to come to the door. *It's not going to work,* she thought over and over as the heat from Griffin's body seeped into hers when he moved behind her. How was she going to pretend to play house with the girls' surrogate father when she could barely tolerate being in the same room with him?

The door opened and Roberta Eaton stood on the other side, her eyes red and swollen. Belinda knew her mother hadn't wanted her granddaughters to leave, but the law was the law and she'd abide by her late daughter's request and the court's decision to have Sabrina and Layla live with Belinda.

"Hi, Mama." Stepping into the entryway, she leaned over and kissed her cheek. "How are the girls?"

Roberta pressed a wrinkled tissue to her nose. "They're much better than I am. But then, you know how adaptable young folks are. I've spent most of the day crying, while they came home going on about an upcoming class trip." Roberta glanced over her daughter's shoulder to find Griffin Rice's broad shoulders filling out the doorway. "Please come in, Griffin."

Griffin moved inside the house with expansive windows and ceilings rising upward to twelve feet. The elder Eatons had downsized, selling their sprawling six-bedroom farmhouse for a two-bedroom town house condo in a newly constructed retirement village. Unlike his parents, who divorced when he was in high school, Dr. Dwight and Roberta Eaton had recently celebrated their forty-second wedding anniversary.

He hadn't remembered a day when his parents did

not argue, which had shaped his views about marriage. His mother said her marriage was a daily struggle, one in which she was always the loser. His father remarried twice and after his last divorce he dated a woman for several years, but ended the relationship when she wanted a more permanent commitment.

When his brother had contacted him with the news that he was getting married, Griffin had at first thought he was joking, because they'd made a vow never to marry. But within three months of meeting Donna Eaton, Grant had tied the knot. At first he had thought his brother wanted a hasty wedding because Donna was pregnant. But his suspicions had been unfounded when the twins were born a year later. When he'd asked Grant about breaking his promise to never marry, his brother had said promises were meant to be broken when you meet the "right" woman.

Griffin dated a lot of women, had had several long-term relationships, yet at thirty-seven he still hadn't found the "right woman."

"Aunt Lindy, Uncle Griff!" Sabrina, older than her sister by two minutes, came bounding down the staircase. "Sorry, Gram," she mumbled when she saw her grandmother's frown.

Her grandmother had lectured her and Layla about acting like young ladies—and that meant walking and not running down the stairs and talking quietly rather than screaming at the top of their lungs.

Belinda held out her arms, and she wasn't disappointed when Sabrina came into her embrace. Easing back, she stared at her niece, always amazed that Sabrina was a younger version of herself. She used to kid Donna by saying that her fraternal twin daughters' genes had been a compromise. Sabrina resembled the Eatons, while Layla was undeniably a Rice.

"How's my favorite girl?"

Sabrina rolled her eyes at the same time she sucked her teeth. "How can I be your favorite when you tell Layla that she's also your favorite?"

Belinda kissed her forehead. "Can't I have two favorite girls?"

Sabrina angled her head, and her expression made her look much older. Not only was she older than Layla, but she was more mature than her twin. She preferred wearing her relaxed shoulder-length hair either loose, or up in a ponytail. It was Layla who'd opted not to cut her hair and fashioned it in a single braid with colorful bands on the end to match her funky, bohemian wardrobe. Both girls had braces to correct an overbite.

"Of course you can," Sabrina said. Pulling away, she went over to Griffin. Standing on tiptoe, she kissed his cheek. "I like your suit."

The charcoal-gray, single-breasted, styled suit in a lightweight wool blend was Griffin's favorite. He tugged her ponytail. "Thank you."

Sabrina gave her uncle a beguiling smile. "You promised that Layla and I could meet Keith Ennis. The Phillies will be in town for four days. Please, please, please, Uncle Griff, can you arrange for us to meet him?"

It was Griffin's turn to roll his eyes. Keith Ennis had become Major League Baseball's latest heartthrob. Groupies greeted him in every city and his official fan club boasted more than a million members online.

He'd considered himself blessed when the batting phenom had approached him to represent him in negotiating his contract when he'd been called up from the minors. The Philadelphia Phillies signed him to a three-year, multimillion-dollar deal that made the rookie one of the highest-paid players in the majors, and in his first year he was named Rookie of the Year, earned a Gold Glove and had hit more than forty home runs with one hundred and ten runs batted in.

"I'm having a gathering at my house next Saturday following an afternoon game. You and your sister can come by early to meet him, but then you have to leave."

"How long can we stay, Uncle Griff?" asked Layla, who'd come down the staircase in time to overhear her uncle.

Belinda shot Griffin an *I don't believe you* look. Had he lost his mind, telling twelve-year-olds that they could come to an adult gathering where there was certain to be not only alcohol, but half-naked hoochies?

"Your uncle and I will have to talk about this before we agree whether an *adult* party is appropriate for twelve-year-olds." She'd deliberately stressed the word *adult*.

Layla pouted as dots of color mottled her clear complexion. "But Uncle Griff said we could go."

"Your uncle doesn't have the final say on where you can go, or what you can do."

"Who does have the final say?" Sabrina asked.

Belinda felt as if she were being set up. Unknowingly, Griffin had made her the bad guy—yet again. "We both will have the final say. Now, please say goodbye to your grandmother. I'd like to get you settled in because tomorrow is a school day."

Most of the girls' clothes and personal belongings had been moved to her house earlier that week. Belinda had hung their clothes in closets but left boxes of stuffed animals and souvenirs for her nieces to unpack and put away.

"We'll see you for Sunday dinner, Gram," Layla promised as she hugged and kissed Roberta.

Roberta gave the girls bear hugs accompanied by grunting sound effects. "I want you to listen to your aunt and uncle, or you'll hear it from me."

"We will, Gram," the two chorused.

Belinda lingered behind as Layla and Sabrina followed Griffin outside. "Why didn't you say something when Griffin mentioned letting the girls hang out at a party with grown folks?"

Roberta crossed her arms under her full bosom and angled her soft, stylishly coiffed salt-and-pepper head. She wanted to tell her middle daughter that becoming a mother was challenging enough, but assuming the responsibility of raising teenage girls, who were still grieving the loss of their parents, and had just started their menses and were subject to mood swings as erratic as the weather, would make her question her sanity.

"I wouldn't permit anyone to interfere with me raising my children, so I'm not going to get into it with you and Griffin about how you want to deal with Layla and Sabrina. Not only are you their aunt but you are also their mother. What you're going to have to do is establish the rules with Griffin before you tell the girls what's expected of them."

Frustration swept over Belinda. Her mother wasn't going to take her side. "I can't understand what made him tell—"

"There's not much to understand, Belinda," Roberta retorted, interrupting her. "He's a man, not a father. What he's going to have to do is begin thinking like a father."

"That's not going to be as easy as it sounds. Layla and Sabrina will spend more time with me than with Griffin. Although he's agreed to take them on the weekends that doesn't mean he'll have them every weekend."

"Griffin Rice is no different than your father. As a family doctor with a private practice he was always on call. If it wasn't a sprained wrist or ankle, then it was the hospital asking him to cover in the E.R. Dwight missed so many Sunday dinners that I stopped setting a place for him at the dinner table."

"Daddy was working, and there is a big difference between working and socializing."

"You can't worry about Griffin, Lindy. Either he will step up to the plate or he won't. At this point in their lives, Sabrina and Layla need a mother not a father. Once the boys start hanging around them, I'm certain he'll change. Your father did."

Belinda wanted to tell her mother that Griffin Rice was nothing like Dwight Eaton. With Griffin it was like sending the fox to guard the henhouse. And, if Griffin didn't take an active role in protecting his nieces now, then she would be forced to be mother *and* father.

"Let's hope you're right." She hugged and kissed her mother. "We'll see you Sunday."

Roberta nodded. "Take care of my girls."

"You know I will, Mama."

Belinda walked out of the house to find Griffin waiting for her. He'd removed his suit jacket, his custom-made shirt and tailored slacks displaying his physique to its best advantage. Sabrina and Layla were seated in the back of the car, bouncing to music blaring from the SUV's speakers. Belinda fixed her gaze on a spot over Griffin's shoulder rather than meet his intense gaze.

There was something about the way he was staring at her that made Belinda slightly uncomfortable. Perhaps it was his earlier reference to her face and body that added to her uneasiness. The first time she was introduced to Griffin Rice she was stunned by his gorgeous face and perfect body, but after interacting with him she'd thought him arrogant and egotistical when he boasted that he'd graduated number one in his law school class.

Subsequent encounters did little to change her opinion of him. Every time the Eatons and Rices got together Griffin flaunted a different woman. After a while, she stopped speaking to him. Even when they came together as godmother and godfather to celebrate their godchildren's birthdays, she never exchanged more than a few words with him.

"We have to talk about the girls, Griffin."

His thick eyebrows arched. "What do you want to talk about?"

"We need to establish some rules concerning parenting."

"I'll go along with whatever you want."

"What I don't want is for you to promise the girls that they can attend an adult party," added Belinda.

"I didn't tell them they could attend the party. I said—"

"I heard what you said, Griffin Rice," Belinda interrupted angrily. "The girls will not go to your house to meet anyone."

Griffin's eyes darkened as he struggled to control his temper. He didn't know what it was about Belinda Eaton, but she was the only woman who managed to annoy him. He'd stopped speaking to her because she

had such a sharp tongue. And rather than argue, he
ignored her. But it was impossible to ignore her now
because he would have to put up with her for the next
eleven years. Once Sabrina and Layla celebrated their
twenty-third birthdays he and Belinda could go their
separate ways. Having his nieces stay at his house on
weekends would put a crimp in his social life, but he was
totally committed to his role as their guardian.

Griffin knew what meeting Keith Ennis and getting
his autograph meant to the girls. His dilemma was
finding a way to get around Belinda's demands. "Are
you willing to compromise?"

"Compromise how?"

"You act as my hostess for the party. Let me finish,"
he warned when she started to open her mouth in
protest. "You and the girls can spend the weekend with
me. You can be my hostess, and I'll ask Keith to come
early so that Sabrina and Layla can meet him. As soon
as the others arrive they can go to their rooms while
you and I—"

"Will meet and greet your guests," Belinda said facetiously, finishing his statement.

Grinning and displaying a mouth filled with straight,
white teeth, Griffin winked at Belinda. "Now, doesn't
that solve everything? The girls get to meet their idol, I
get to interact with my friends and clients and you will
be there to monitor Sabrina and Layla."

*I don't think the girls need as much monitoring as
you do,* Belinda mused. "I hope when the girls stay over
that you won't expose them to situations they don't
need to see at their age."

It took a full minute for Griffin to discern what
Belinda was implying. "Do you really believe I'm so

depraved that I would sleep with a woman when my
nieces are in the same house?"

"I don't know what to believe, Griffin." Belinda's
voice was pregnant with sarcasm. "What you're going
to have to do is prove to me that you're capable of
looking after two pre-teen girls."

"I don't have to prove anything to you, Belinda. The
fact that my brother thought me worthy enough to care
for and protect his daughters is enough. And, regardless
of what you may think—legally I have as much right to
see my nieces as you do. I agreed to let them stay with
you during the week because their school is in the same
district where you live. It would be detrimental to their
stability to pull them out midterm to go to a school
close to where I live."

He took a step, bringing him within inches of his
sister-in-law, his gaze lingering on the delicate features
that made for an arresting face. What he hadn't wanted
to acknowledge the first time he was introduced to
Belinda Eaton was that she was stunningly beautiful.
She had it all: looks and brains. Also, what he refused
to think about was her lithe, curvy body. The one time
he saw her in a bikini he'd found himself transfixed by
what had been concealed by her conservative attire. It
took weeks before the image of her long, shapely legs
and the soft excess of flesh rising above her bikini top
faded completely. That had been the first and only time
that Griffin Rice was consciously aware that he wanted
to make love to Belinda Eaton.

"Okay, Griffin. I'll compromise just this one time.
But only because I don't want to disappoint Layla and
Sabrina."

Griffin smiled, the expression softening his face

and making him even more attractive. "Why, thank you, Belinda."

Belinda also smiled. "You're quite welcome, Griffin."

Chapter 2

"Aren't you coming in with us, Uncle Griff?" Sabrina asked as Griffin stood on the porch of Belinda's two-story white house framed with dark blue molding and matching shutters.

Cupping the back of her head, Griffin pressed a kiss to her forehead. "I can't. I have a prior engagement."

Sabrina blinked once. "You're engaged?"

Throwing back his head, Griffin laughed. "No. I should've said that I have a dinner appointment."

"Why didn't you say that instead of saying you were engaged," Sabrina countered, not seeing the humor in her uncle's statement.

Griffin sobered quickly when he realized she wasn't amused. Everyone remarked how Sabrina had an old spirit, that she was wise beyond her years, while Layla the free spirit saw goodness in everything and everyone.

"It looks as if I'm going to have to be very careful about what I say to you."

Sabrina winked at him. "That's all right, Uncle Griff. I'll let you know when I don't understand something."

Belinda listened to the exchange between Griffin and his niece. It was apparent he'd met his match. "If you're not coming in, then I'll say good night."

Watching him drive away, she was grateful that Griffin had elected not to come inside because she wanted time alone with her nieces, to see firsthand their reaction to the rooms she'd organized and decorated in what she felt was each girl's personal style.

Belinda glanced at her watch. "Girls, please go upstairs, do your homework and then get ready for bed. I'm going to have to get you up earlier than usual because I'm going to drive you to school. I also have to fill out another transportation application changing your bus route." The sisters headed for the staircase, racing each other to the second floor.

Their bus route had changed when they'd gone to live with their grandparents, and it would change again now that they lived with her. It'd taken Belinda two months for the contractor to make the necessary renovations to her house when she realized the twins would have to live with her. She hadn't known that when she'd moved out of her Philadelphia co-op and into the three-bedroom house. She'd originally bought the house because she'd been looking to live in a less noisy neighborhood with a slower pace. Now she would end up sharing the house with her nieces.

The house's former owners, a childless couple who taught in the same high school as Belinda, had covered the clapboard with vinyl siding, updated the plumbing and electricity and had landscaped the entire property as they awaited the adoption of a child from Eastern Europe. The adoption fell through and the wife opted for artificial insemination. After several failed tries, she found herself pregnant with not one, but four babies. They began looking for a larger house at the same time Belinda put her co-op on the market. She made the couple an offer, and three months later she closed on what had become her little dream house.

Ear-piercing screams floated down from the second story. Glancing up, she saw Layla hanging over the banister. "Are you okay?" she asked with a smile, knowing the reason for the screaming.

Layla gestured wildly. "Aunt Lindy, I love, love, *love* it!" she shrieked incoherently before running back to her bedroom.

Minutes later Belinda stood in the room, her arms encircling her nieces' waists. The contractor had removed the door leading into the master bedroom and installed doors to adjoining bedrooms that led directly into the space she'd set up as a combined office, study and entertainment area. The furnishings included two desks with chairs that faced each other and built-in bookcases along three of the four walls.

The remaining wall held a large flat-screen television. A low table held electronics for a home-theater system. Empty racks for CDs and DVDs were nestled in a corner, along with a worktable with a streamlined desktop and laptop computers and printer. Although the television was equipped with cable, Belinda had programmed parental controls on both the television and

Internet. French doors had replaced a trio of windows
that led to a balcony overlooking the back of the property.

"I know which bedroom is mine," Sabrina crooned.

"Mine is the one with the bright colors," Layla said,
her voice rising in excitement.

Sabrina pressed closer to her aunt. "This is the first
time we're not going to have to share a bedroom."

Belinda gave her a warm smile. She recognized them
as individuals and sought to relate to them as such. "I
have a few house rules that I expect to be followed. You
must keep your bedrooms and bathroom clean. I don't
want to find dirty clothes on the floor or under the beds.
The first time I find food or drink upstairs there will be
consequences."

Layla shot her a questioning glance. "What kind of
consequences?"

"There will be no television or Internet for a week. The
only exception is to do homework. You'll also have to give
up your iPods and relinquish your cell phones—"

"But we don't have cell phones," Sabrina interrupted,
sharing a look with her sister.

A mysterious smile tipped the corners of Belinda's
mouth. "If you look in the drawer of your bedside tables
you'll find a cell phone. The phones are a gift from
your uncle Griffin. He's programmed the numbers
where you can reach him or me in an emergency. You'll
share a thousand minutes each month, plus unlimited
texting. You…"

Her words trailed off when the girls raced out of the
room, leaving her staring at the spots where they'd been.

She'd turned the master bedroom into a sanctuary for
her nieces, decorated Sabrina's room with a queen-size,
off-white sleigh bed, with matching dresser, nightstands

and lingerie chest. Waning daylight filtered through sheer curtains casting shadows on the white comforter dotted with embroidered yellow-and-green butterflies. Layla's room reflected her offbeat style and personality with orange-red furniture and earth-toned accessories.

Belinda had moved her own bedroom to the first floor in what had been the enclosed back porch. It faced southeast, which meant the rising sun rather than an alarm clock woke her each morning. Layla and Sabrina returned, clutching Sidekick cell phones while doing the "happy dance."

"Girls, I want you in bed by nine."

"Yes, Aunt Lindy," they said in unison.

She walked out of the study and made her way down the carpeted hallway to the staircase. Giving her nieces the run of the second floor would serve two purposes: it would give them a measure of independence and make them responsible for keeping their living space clean.

Griffin couldn't remember the last time a woman had bored him to the point of walking out on a date. However, he'd promised Renata Crosby that he would have dinner with her the next time she came to Philadelphia on business. The screenwriter was pretty, but that's where her appeal started and ended. From the time she sat down at the table in one of his favorite restaurants, Renata had talked nonstop about how much money she'd lost because of the writer's strike in Hollywood. He wanted to tell her that everyone affected by the strike lost money.

"Griffin, darling, you haven't heard a word I've been saying," Renata admonished softly.

Griffin forced his attention back to the woman with

eyes the color of lapis lazuli. Their deep blue color was the perfect foil for her olive complexion and straight raven-black, chin-length hair.

"I'm sorry," he mumbled apologetically, "but my mind is elsewhere."

Renata blinked, a fringe of lashes touching the ridge of high cheekbones. She'd spent the better part of an hour trying to seduce Griffin Rice, but it was apparent her scheme to get him to sleep with her wasn't working. She'd met the highly successful and charismatic sports attorney at an L.A. hot spot, and knew within seconds that she had to have a piece of him.

At the time, he was scheduled to fly out of LAX for the East Coast. So she had followed him to the parking lot where a driver waited for him and got him to exchange business cards with her. She and Griffin had played phone tag for more than a month until one day he answered his phone. She told him that she was meeting a client in Philadelphia, and wanted to have dinner with him before flying back to California. Of course, there was no client and it appeared as if she'd flown three thousand miles for nothing.

"You do seem rather distracted," she crooned, deliberately lowering her voice.

Griffin stared at his fingers splayed over the pristine, white tablecloth. "That's because it isn't every day that a man becomes the father of twin girls."

An audible gasp escaped Renata. "You're a father?"

Griffin angled his head and smiled. "Awesome, isn't it?"

Pressing her lips together, Renata swallowed hard. When she'd inquired about Griffin Rice's marital status she was told that he wasn't married. Had her source lied, or had Griffin perfected the art of keeping his private life *very* private?

"I'd say it's downright shocking. You didn't know your wife was having twins?"

"I'm not married."

"If you're not married, then you're a baby daddy. Or should I say a *babies'* daddy."

Griffin registered the contempt in Renata's voice. Although he wasn't remotely interested in her, he was still perturbed by her reaction. After all, he'd only agreed to have dinner with her to be polite. Raising his hand, he signaled for the check.

"I'm going to forget you said that."

Renata concealed her embarrassment behind a too-bright smile. "I'm sorry it came out that way. Please, let me make it up to you by sending you something for your girls," she said in an attempt to salvage what was left of her pride.

"Apology accepted, but no, thank you." He signed the check, pushed back his chair to come around the table and help Renata. When she came to her feet, he offered, "Can I drop you anywhere?"

Renata was nearly eye to eye with Griffin in her heels. She knew they would've made a striking couple if some other woman hadn't gotten her hooks into him. She'd met more Griffin Rices than she could count on both hands. Most were good-looking, high-profile men who were willing to be seen with women like her, but when all was said and done they married women who wouldn't cheat on them, or whom other men wouldn't give a second glance. As soon as she returned to her hotel room she planned to call an entertainment reporter and give him the lowdown about Griffin Rice having fathered twins.

"No, thanks. I have a rental outside."

He took her arm. "I'll walk you to your car."

Griffin gave Renata the obligatory kiss on the cheek, waited until she maneuvered out of the restaurant's parking lot and then made his way to where he'd parked his car. He wasn't as annoyed with Renata's inane conversation as he was with himself for wasting three precious hours he could've spent with his nieces. Glancing at the watch strapped to his wrist, he noted the time. It was eight thirty-five, and he wanted to talk to Sabrina and Layla before they went to bed for the night.

He exceeded the speed limit to make it to Belinda's house in record time. She'd bought a house a mile from where Grant and Donna had lived, the perfect neighborhood for upwardly mobile young couples with children. Grant had tried to convince him to purchase one of the newer homes of the McMansion variety, but Griffin preferred the charm of the nineteenth-century homes along the Main Line. Though less exclusive than it once was, the suburb west of the city was still identified with the crème de la crème of Philadelphia society.

Whenever he closed the door to his three-story colonial on a half-acre lot along the tree-lined street in Paoli, he was no longer the hard-nosed negotiator trying to make the best deal for his client. Sitting on his patio overlooking a picturesque landscape of massive century-old trees and a carpet of wildflowers had become his ultimate pleasure. He opened his home on average about three times a year to entertain family, friends and clients. Living in Paoli suited his temperament. After growing up in a crowded, bustling Philadelphia neighborhood he'd come to appreciate the quietness of the suburb of fifty-four hundred residents.

Griffin maneuvered into Belinda's wide driveway and shut off the engine. His dark mood lifted when he saw soft light coming through the first-floor windows. It was apparent Belinda hadn't gone to bed. He rang the bell, waited and raised his hand to ring it again when the door opened and he came face-to-face with Belinda as she dabbed her face with a hand towel. Judging from her expression it was apparent that she was as shocked to see him as he to see her in a pair of shorts and a re-vealing tank top. And, with her freshly scrubbed face and headband that pulled her hair off her face, she appeared no older than the high school students to whom she taught American history.

"What are you doing here?" Belinda asked, her voice a breathless whisper.

Leaning against the doorframe, Griffin stared at the rise and fall of her breasts under the cotton fabric. He swallowed a groan when a part of his body reacted in-voluntarily to the wanton display of skin.

"I came to see if the...my daughters are okay."

Belinda was surprised to hear Griffin refer to his nieces as his daughters. It was apparent he intended to take sur-rogate parenting seriously. "Of course they're okay, Griffin. If you hadn't run off you would've known that."

Griffin straightened. "I had a prior engagement."

She rolled her eyes at him. "Call it what it is."

"And that is?"

"You had a date, Griffin."

A slow, sexy smile found its way over Griffin's face. "Do I detect a modicum of jealousy, Eaton?"

"Surely you jest, Rice. Let me assure you I'm not at-tracted to you, and there's nothing about you that I find even remotely appealing."

Griffin brushed past her, walking into the entryway. "Sheath your claws, Belinda. What you should do is channel your frustration in an anger management seminar because we're going to have to deal with each other until the girls celebrate their twenty-third birthday. You don't like me and I have to admit that you're certainly not at the top of the list for what I want in a woman."

Belinda affected a brittle smile. "At least we can agree on one thing."

"And that is?" he asked, lifting his expressive eyebrows.

"We won't interfere in each other's love lives."

"You're seeing someone?"

"Does that surprise you, Griffin?" she asked, answering his question with one of her own.

Belinda's revelation that she was involved with a man came as a shock to Griffin. He never saw her with a man, so he'd assumed that she spent her nights at home—alone. "I hope you're not going to schedule sleep-overs with *your* man now that the girls are living with you. It wouldn't set a good example—"

"He'll only come when the girls stay at your place," she interrupted.

Griffin didn't know where he'd gotten the notion that Belinda wasn't seeing anyone. Although he would never admit to her that he was attracted to her in *that way,* it didn't mean that other men weren't. Earlier, he'd sat watching Jonathan Connelly unable to take his eyes off her. And Griffin didn't blame the man because Belinda Eaton was stunning.

If she hadn't been so unapproachable he would've considered asking her out. Even when they'd come together as best man and maid of honor for the wedding of their respective siblings, he'd thought her shy and reticent. But then he hadn't expected more from a nineteen-year-old college student who'd lived on campus her first semester, then without warning moved back home, driving more than thirty miles each day to attend classes. When asked why she'd opted not to stay on campus, her response was as enigmatic as the woman she'd become.

Griffin remembered why he'd come to Belinda's house. "May I see the girls?"

"I'm sorry. They've already gone to bed."

He glanced at the clock on the table filled with potted plants. "It's only nine-fifteen. Isn't that a little early?"

"No, it isn't, Griffin. My mother had a problem with getting them up on school days, so I've instituted a nine o'clock curfew Sunday through Thursday and eleven on Fridays and Saturdays."

"That sounds a little strict, Belinda."

"Children need structure."

"Structure is one thing and being on lockdown is another."

Belinda walked around Griffin and opened the door wider. "I don't want to be rude, but you really need to go home, Griffin. I'm going to be up late grading papers, and hopefully I'll be able to get a few hours of sleep before I have to get up earlier than usual to drive the girls to school. I need to stop in the school office to update their emergency contact numbers and bus route."

After seeing that Layla and Sabrina had completed their homework, she'd eaten leftovers, applied a facial masque and sat in a tub of warm water waiting for it to set. By the time she'd emerged from the bathroom the girls had come to kiss her good-night. They'd gone to bed, while she would probably be up well past midnight.

Griffin heard something in Belinda's voice that he'd never recognized before: defeat. Although they shared custody of their nieces, it was Belinda who'd assumed most of the responsibility for caring for them five of the seven days a week. And for the weeks when he had to travel on business, it would be the entire week.

"What time do your classes begin?"

"Eight. But I have a sub filling in for me."

Griffin knew he had to help Belinda or she would find herself in over her head. It was one thing to raise a child from infancy and another thing completely when you found yourself having to deal with not one but two teenagers with very strong personalities.

"Let me help you out."

Belinda stared at the man standing in her entryway as if he were a stranger. "*You* want to help *me*."

Slipping his hands into the pockets of his suit trousers, Griffin angled his head. "Yes. I'll take the girls to school and take care of the paperwork. That way you don't have to have to miss your classes."

"It's too late to cancel the substitute."

Attractive lines fanned out around his eyes when he gave her a warm smile. "Use the extra time to sleep in late."

His smile was contagious as Belinda returned it with one of her own. "It sounds good, but I still have to get up and prepare breakfast."

"Can't they get breakfast at school?"

"Donna wouldn't let them eat school breakfast because they weren't eating enough fiber."

"I'll fix breakfast for them," Griffin volunteered.

"It can't be fast food."

He winked at her. "I didn't know you were a comedian.

Why would I give them a fast-food breakfast when it has a higher caloric content and more preservatives than some cafeteria food? I'll cook breakfast for them."

Belinda hesitated, processing what she'd just heard. "You're going to come here from Paoli tomorrow morning in time to make breakfast and take the girls to school?" The ongoing family joke was that Griffin Rice would be late for his own funeral.

"Yes."

Belinda waved a hand. "Forget it, Griffin. I'll get up and make breakfast *and* take them to school."

"You doubt whether I'll be here on time?"

She leaned closer. "I know you won't make it."

The warmth and the subtle scent of lavender on Belinda's bared flesh wafted in Griffin's nostrils, making him more than aware of her blatant femininity. For years he'd told himself that he didn't like his sister-in-law because she was a snob—that her attitude was that she was too good for him because she came from a more prestigious family.

But in the past four months he saw another side of Belinda Eaton that hadn't been apparent in the dozen years since they first met. Not only was she generous, but also selfless in her attempt to become a surrogate mother for her sister's children. She had reconfigured the design of her house to accommodate the teenage girls. He hadn't known she had a man in her life, and apparently that relationship would also change now that Layla and Sabrina were living with her.

"I'll make it if I stay over."

"You can't stay here," Belinda said quickly. "Have you forgotten that I no longer have an extra bedroom?"

She'd turned the master bedroom into the office/entertainment retreat for the twins and added half baths to the two remaining bedrooms. There was still a full bathroom on the second floor and a half bath off the kitchen, but with three females living under one roof everyone needed a bathroom to call their own.

Griffin affected a Cheshire cat grin. "I can always sleep with you."

Belinda stared at him as if he'd lost his mind. "You're crazy as hell if you think I'm going to let you sleep in my bed with me."

"And why not?" he asked quietly. "Aren't we family, Aunt Lindy?"

"First of all I'm not your aunt. And secondly, you and I don't share blood, therefore we're not family. If you want to stay over then you're going to have to sleep in the living room on the sofa. It converts to a queen-size bed and the mattress is very comfortable."

"How would you know it's comfortable?"

"I slept on it before my bedroom was completed." Although she'd moved her bedroom from the second to the first floor she liked her new space because it was larger, airy and filled with an abundance of light during daytime hours.

Griffin nodded. "I'll take your word that it's comfortable, but if I wake up with a bad back then I'm going to hold you responsible for my medical expenses."

"You won't need a chiropractor after I walk on your back," Belinda countered confidently. "My feet and toes are magical."

He glanced down at her slender pedicured feet in a pair of thong slippers. Her feet were like the rest of her body—perfect. Belinda Eaton was physically perfect, yet so untouchable. He wondered about the man who'd managed to get next to her. There was no doubt he was nothing less than Mister Perfect himself.

"We'll see," he replied noncommittally. "I'm going to head out to Paoli, get a few things. Are you sure you'll be up when I get back?"

"I have an extra set of keys you can use."

"What about your alarm?"

"I won't set it."

"Set it," Griffin ordered. "I'd feel better knowing you and the girls are protected by a silent alarm before I get back. Now, give me the password. Please," he added when Belinda glared at him. He repeated it a couple of times aloud, then to himself. "I'll bring back a set of keys to my place for you, and I'll give you my password."

Belinda turned and walked in the direction of the kitchen where she retrieved a set of keys to her house from a utility drawer. She returned to find Griffin standing in the middle of her living room staring at photographs on tables and lining the fireplace mantel. His gaze was fixed on one of himself, Grant and Donna together at an Eaton-Rice family picnic. It'd taken her weeks to come to grips that her sister and brother-in-law were gone and that she would never hear their laughter again. She'd put away all of their photographs, then caught herself when she realized that if she wanted to remember them, it would be best to see them smiling and happy.

"Griffin."

Griffin turned when Belinda called his name, his expression mirroring the sadness and pain that returned when he least expected it. There had only been he and Grant, the two of them inseparable. Grant was two years older, but he never seemed to mind that he had to take his younger brother everywhere he went.

They were always there for each other throughout their triumphs and failures. Grant was gone, but his spirit for life lived on in the daughters he had called his "princesses." Grant had asked him whether he'd take care of his "princesses" if anything ever happened to him and Griffin hadn't hesitated when he said *of course,* unaware that a decade later he would be called upon to do just that. Grant had also revealed that Belinda Eaton had agreed to share guardianship of his children with him. He'd always thought Donna's younger sister was shy and very pretty, but that had been the extent of his awareness of the young woman who'd been Donna's maid of honor at his brother's wedding.

Now standing several feet away wasn't a shy, pretty girl but a very confident, beautiful woman who always seemed confrontational, something he'd never accept from other women. But he had to remember that Belinda Eaton wasn't just any woman. She was now the mother and he the father to their twin nieces.

"Yes?"

Belinda held out her hand. "Here are your keys." He took the keys suspended from a colorful Lucite souvenir from Hershey Park. "I'll make up the sofa and leave a light on for you."

Griffin nodded. "Thank you. I'll lock the door and set the alarm on my way out."

Belinda was still standing in the middle of the living room when she heard the soft beep that signaled that the alarm was being armed. In another forty-five seconds it would be activated.

Today she'd spent more time with Griffin Rice than she had since planning and rehearsing for her sister's wedding. Her opinion of him hadn't changed over the years. She still found him outspoken, brash and a skirt-chaser. What had changed was that she saw for the first time that he truly loved his nieces. His reference to Sabrina and Layla as his daughters really shocked her, and his volunteering to take them to school was a blessing. He'd stepped up to the plate much sooner than she'd expected he would.

Perhaps, she thought as she made her way upstairs to the linen closet, Griffin did have some redeeming qualities after all. What she didn't want to linger on was how good he looked and smelled. He'd removed his tie and jacket and when she opened the door to find him standing there in just a shirt and trousers she discovered that her pulse beat a little too quickly for her to be un-affected by his presence, and at that moment she knew she was no different than the thousands of other women who lusted after the sports attorney who'd become a celebrity in his own right.

What Belinda had to do was be careful—be very, very careful not to fall victim to his looks and potent charm.

Chapter 3

Belinda woke as daylight filtered through layers of silk panels covering the French doors. Every piece of furniture and all the accessories in her bedroom were in varying shades of white. The absence of color in the bedroom was offset by the calming blue shades in an adjoining sitting/dressing room. Blue-and-white striped cushions on a white chaise, where she spent hours reading and grading papers, and a blue-and-white checked tablecloth on a small table with two pull-up chairs were where she usually enjoyed a late-night cup of coffee and took her breakfast on weekend mornings.

Stretching her arms above her head, she smiled when the sounds of birds singing and chirping to one another shattered the early-morning solitude. It was spring, the clocks were on daylight savings time and she'd spent the winter waiting for longer days and warmer weather after a brutally cold and snowy winter season. Rolling over on her side, she peered at the clock on the bedside table. It was six-thirty—the same time she woke every morning.

She'd just gotten into bed when she heard Griffin come in around midnight. She didn't know why, but the notion of whether he slept nude, in pajamas or in his underwear made her laugh until she pulled a pillow over her head to muffle the sound. That was her last thought before she fell into a deep, dreamless slumber.

Sitting up, she swung her legs over the side of the bed and reached for the wrap on the nearby chair. Today was Thursday and she had a standing appointment with her hairdresser. Wednesdays were set aside for a manicure and pedicure and she planned to ask her nieces if they wanted to accompany her.

The house was quiet as she took the back staircase to the full bathroom on the second floor. Belinda hadn't wanted to walk past the living room where Griffin slept. Her feet were muffled by the hallway runner as she made her way past the closed doors to Sabrina's and Layla's bedrooms. She'd told the girls to set their alarms, because she wasn't going to be responsible for waking them up. Like Griffin, they also liked to sleep in late. It had to be a Rice trait.

Belinda didn't linger. Having completed her morning routine, she left the bathroom the way she'd come, encountering the smell of brewing coffee. A knowing smile parted her lips. Griffin was up.

By the time she'd made up her bed, slipped into a pair of faded jeans, T-shirt and brushed her hair, securing it into a ponytail, the sound of footsteps echoed over her head. It was apparent her nieces had gotten up without her assistance. Donna had made it a practice to wake them up and the habit continued with Roberta.

When she and Donna were that age, Roberta had insisted that they set their alarm clocks in order to get up in plenty of time to ready themselves for school. Griffin had accused her of being rigid, while she thought of it as preparation for the future. No one would be coming to their homes to wake them up so they could make it to work on time.

Belinda walked into the kitchen to find Griffin transferring buckwheat pancakes from the stovetop grill onto a platter. The white T-shirt and jeans riding low on his slim hips made her breath catch in her throat. Her gaze was drawn to the muscles in his biceps that flexed with every motion. She regarded Griffin as a skirt-chaser, but after seeing him moving around her kitchen as if he'd done it countless times she realized he would be a good catch for some woman—provided he would be faithful to her.

"Good morning."

Griffin glanced up, smiling. "Well, good morning to you, too."

Belinda walked into the kitchen and sat on a high stool at the cooking island. "I didn't know you could cook."

He winked at her. "That's because you don't know me."

She decided not to respond to his declaration. "How's your back?" Belinda asked instead.

"Good. Remember when you banish your man to the couch that it's not going to be much of a punishment."

"When I have to put a man out of my bed he won't end up on the couch but on the *sidewalk*." She'd stressed the last word.

Griffin grimaced. "Ouch!"

Belinda slipped off the stool. "Do you want me to help you with anything?"

"I stopped at a twenty-four-hour green grocer and bought some fruit. I put it in the refrigerator, but if you prepare it for me I'd really appreciate it."

Working side by side, Belinda washed and cut melon, strawberries and pineapple into small pieces for a fresh fruit salad while Griffin finished making pancakes. When Sabrina and Layla came downstairs, dressed in their school uniforms—white blouse, gray pleated skirt and gray blazer and knee socks—the kitchen was redolent with different flavors of fruit, freshly squeezed orange juice, pancakes and coffee for Belinda and Griffin. There was only the sound of a newscaster's voice coming from the radio on a countertop as the four ate breakfast.

"I have an appointment for my hair this afternoon," Belinda said, breaking the comfortable silence. She looked at Sabrina, then Layla. "Who would like to go with me?"

"I do," Sabrina said.

"Me, too," Layla chimed in.

"I'll pick you up from school, and we'll go directly from there to the salon. Make certain you bring your books so you can do your homework while under the dryer. Thursday is girls' night out, so let me know where you'd like to eat."

Belinda's last class would end at two and the twins weren't dismissed until three. The half-hour drive would afford her more than enough time to pick them up. However, if she ran into traffic, then she could call her mother to have her meet them. Layla peered over her glass at her uncle. "Even though it's for girls, can Uncle Griff eat with us?"

Belinda stared at Griffin, silently admiring his close-cropped hair and the smoothness of his clean-shaven jaw. Mixed feelings surged through her as she tried to read the man sitting in her kitchen who continued to show her that there was more to Griffin Rice than photo ops with pro athletes, A-list actors and entertainment celebrities. His success in negotiating multimillion-dollar contracts for athletes was noteworthy, while his reputation for dating supermodels and actresses was legendary. A tabloid ran a story documenting the names of the women and a time line of his numerous relationships—most of which averaged six to nine months.

"I can't answer for him, Layla."

She smiled at her uncle. "Can you eat with us, Uncle Griff?"

Dropping an arm over Layla's shoulders, Griffin kissed her mussed hair. "I can't, baby girl. I'm going to see my folks before they leave on vacation."

In their shared grief over losing their firstborn, his parents had become at sixty what they hadn't been in their twenties—friends. Now they were embarking on a month-long European cruise they'd always planned to take for their fortieth wedding anniversary. Lucas and Gloria Rice's marriage hadn't survived two decades. However, both were older, wiser and sensible enough to know they couldn't change the past, so were willing to make the best of the present.

"When are Grandma and Grandpa coming back?" Sabrina asked.

"They won't be back until the beginning of May." Griffin stared at the clock on the microwave.

Layla wiped her mouth with a napkin. "Are you going to fix breakfast for us tomorrow, Uncle Griff?"

"Your aunt and I agreed you would spend the weekends with me, and that means I'll make breakfast for you Saturday and Sunday mornings."

"I hope you don't expect me to make pancakes every day, but I'll definitely make certain your breakfasts will be healthy," Belinda said when the two girls gave her long, penetrating stares. "As soon as you're finished here I want you to comb your hair. Your uncle will drive you to school this morning."

A frown formed between Layla's eyes. She appeared as if she'd been in a wrestling match, with tufts of hair standing out all over her head. "I thought the bus was picking us up."

Belinda stood up and began clearing the table. "Griffin will fill out the paperwork today changing your official address to this house. As soon as it's approved, you'll be put on the bus route."

"Layla's boyfriend rides the bus," Sabrina crooned in a singsong tone.

A rush of color darkened Layla's face, concealing the sprinkle of freckles dotting her pert nose. "No, he doesn't!" she screamed as Griffin and Belinda exchanged shocked glances. "Breena is a liar!"

Resting his elbows on the table, Griffin supported his chin on a closed fist. "Do you have a boyfriend, Layla?" His voice, though soft, held a thread of steel.

Layla's eyes filled with tears. "Stop them, Aunt Lindy."

Belinda felt her heart turn over. Her sensitive, free-spirited niece was hurting and she knew what Layla was going through, because she'd experienced her first serious crush on a boy in her class the year she turned twelve. She'd confided her feelings to her best friend and before the end of the day everyone in the entire school, including Daniel Campbell, knew she liked him.

"If Layla likes a boy, then that's her business, not ours."

Griffin sat up straighter. "She's too young to have a boyfriend."

"But I don't have a boyfriend," Layla sobbed, as tears trickled down her cheeks.

Belinda rounded on Griffin. "Griffin, you're upsetting the child. She says she doesn't have a boyfriend." She held up a hand when he opened his mouth. "We'll talk about this later. Sabrina and Layla, I want you to finish your breakfast then please go and comb your hair. And don't forget what I said yesterday about leaving clothes on the floor."

Layla sprang up from the table, leaving her twin staring at her back. Sabrina closed her eyes. "I didn't mean to make her cry."

Belinda shook her head. "If you didn't mean it then you shouldn't have said what you said. Remember, Sabrina, that your words *and* actions have consequences."

Nodding, Sabrina pushed back her chair. "I'll tell her I'm sorry."

Belinda closed her eyes for several seconds and when she opened them she found Griffin glaring at her. "What?"

"The girls can't date until they're eighteen."

"Are you asking me or telling me, Griffin?"

He stared, not blinking. "I'm only making a suggestion."

"I believe seventeen would be more appropriate."

"Why?"

"By that time they'll be in their last year of high school and that will give them a year to deal with the ups and downs of what they'll believe is love. Then once they're in college they'll be used to the lies and tricks dogs masquerading as men perpetuate so well."

Griffin's expressive eyebrows shot up. "You think all men are dogs?"

Belinda rinsed and stacked dishes in the dishwasher. "If the shoe fits, then wear it, Griffin Rice. If a woman dated as many men as you do women, people would call her a whore."

"I don't date that many women."

"Why, then, didn't you sue that tabloid that documented your many trysts?"

"I don't have the time, nor the inclination to keep up with gossip."

Resting a hip against the counter, Belinda gave him a long, penetrating stare. "Are you saying what they printed wasn't true?"

There came a lengthy pause before Griffin said, "Yes."

"What about the photographs of you and different women?"

"They were photo ops."

"They were photo ops for whose benefit?"

"Most times for the lady."

"So, all that dishing about you being a womanizer is bogus."

Leaning on his elbow, Griffin cradled his chin in his hand. "If I'd slept with as many women as the tabloids claim I have I doubt whether I'd be able to stand up."

Belinda turned her head to conceal her smile. "Real or imaginary, you're going to have to clean up your image now that you're a father."

Now that you're a father.

Belinda's words were branded into Griffin's consciousness as he got up to take the rest of the dishes off the table. He, who hadn't wanted to marry and become a father because he didn't want his children to go through what he'd experienced with his warring parents, now at thirty-seven, found himself playing daddy to his adolescent nieces.

When Jonathan Connolly had called to tell him that he had received the documents legalizing the girls' adoption, Griffin felt his heart stop before it started up again. He'd feared his life would change so dramatically, that he would have to hire a nanny to take care of his nieces and that he wouldn't be able to recognize who he was or what he'd become until he remembered Belinda telling him she would have the girls live with her, and if he chose he could have them on weekends.

Belinda's suggestion had come as a shock to him. He'd thought of her as the consummate career woman. She taught high school history, spent her winter vacations in the Caribbean or Florida and traveled abroad during the summer months.

He had vacillated between indifference and new-found respect for Belinda when she'd decided to renovate her house to address the needs and interests of the two children she'd thought of as her own within days of them losing their parents.

Belinda Eaton had sacrificed her day-to-day existence for "her children" while he hadn't given up anything. When he'd come to her house the night before he said he'd come to see his children. They weren't only his children or Belinda's children. Sabrina and Layla Rice were now legally the children of both Belinda Eaton and Griffin Rice.

"I'll try, Belinda."

She gave him a level look. "Don't try, Griffin. Just do it."

He nodded in a gesture of acquiescence. "I'm going to change my clothes. I want to get to the school early enough so I don't have to wait to be seen."

Belinda turned back to finish cleaning up the kitchen. She didn't have to be at the high school until eleven, which left her time to dust and vacuum. As the only person living in the house her house was always spotless. But she knew that was going to change because Donna hadn't taught her daughters to pick up after themselves.

As a stay-at-home mother and housewife Donna didn't mind picking up after her husband and children. Roberta Eaton had picked up after her four children, and Donna continued the practice. However, that would end with Belinda. As a certifiable neat-freak, the girls would either conform to her standards or they would forfeit their privileges.

She'd loaded the dishwasher and had begun sweeping the kitchen when Sabrina and Layla walked in with backpacks slung over their shoulders. Both had combed and neatly braided their hair into single plaits. The fuzzy hair around their hairline was evidence that it was time for their roots to be touched up.

"Before you ask, Aunt Lindy, we brushed our teeth," Sabrina announced with a teasing smile.

Resting her hands on her denim-covered hips, Belinda looked at her from under lowered lids. "I wasn't going to ask, Miss Prissy."

"Who's prissy?" asked a deep voice. Griffin stood at the entrance to the kitchen dressed in a lightweight navy blue suit, stark white shirt, striped silk tie and black leather slip-ons.

Belinda couldn't contain the soft gasp escaping her parted lips as she stared at Griffin like a star-struck teen seeing her idol in person for the first time. Now she knew why women came on to Griffin Rice. He radiated masculinity like radioactive particles transmitting deadly rays. Her knees buckled slightly as she held on to the broom handle to keep her balance.

A nervous smile trembled over her lips. "Your daughter."

Smiling, Griffin strolled into the kitchen. "Which one?"

"Sabrina," Belinda and Layla said in unison, before touching fists.

Looping his arm around Sabrina's neck, Griffin lowered his head and kissed her forehead. "Are you being prissy, Miss Rice?"

Tilting her chin, she smiled up at her uncle. "I don't even know what prissy means."

He ran a finger down the length of her short nose. "Look it up in the dictionary."

Sabrina snapped her fingers. "How did I know you were going to say that?"

"That's because you're smart."

Belinda propped the broom against the back of a chair. "Come give me a kiss before you leave."

She hugged and kissed Sabrina, then Layla. "Remember we have hair appointments this afternoon."

"Yes!" they said in unison.

Griffin shook his head. He didn't know what it was about women getting their hair and nails done that elicited so much excitement. He got his hair cut every two weeks, but he didn't feel any different after he left the hair salon than when he entered.

"Girls, please wait outside for me. I'll be right out after I talk to your aunt."

Belinda didn't, couldn't move as Griffin approached her. The sensual scent of his aftershave washed over her, and she was lost, lost in a spell of the sexy man who made her feel things she didn't want to feel and made her want him even when she'd openly confessed that she hadn't found him appealing.

She'd lied.

She'd lied to Griffin.

And she'd lied to herself.

"What do you want, Griffin?" Her query had come out in a breathless whisper, as if she were winded from running.

He took another step, bringing them only inches apart. "I just wanted to say goodbye and hope you have a wonderful day."

She blinked. "You didn't have to send the girls out to tell me that."

"But I couldn't do this in front of them," he said cryptically.

"Do what?"

"Do this." Griffin's arm wrapped around her waist, pulling her flush against his body at the same time his mouth covered hers.

Belinda didn't have time to respond to the feel of his masculine mouth on hers as she attempted to push him away. Then the kiss changed as his lips became persuasive, coaxing and gentle. Her arms moved up of their own volition and curled around his neck, and she found herself matching him kiss for kiss. Then it ended as quickly as it had begun.

Reaching up, Griffin eased her arms from around his

neck, his gaze narrowing when he stared at her swollen mouth. Passion had darkened her eyes until no light could penetrate them. Belinda had called Sabrina prissy, when it was she who was prissy. And underneath her prissy schoolteacher exterior was a very passionate woman, and he wondered if her boyfriend knew what he had.

"Thank you for the kiss. You've just made my day." Turning on his heels, he walked across the kitchen, a grin spreading across his face.

"I didn't kiss you, Griffin," Belinda threw at his broad back. "Remember, you kissed me."

He stopped but didn't turn around. "But you kissed me back."

"No, I didn't."

"Yeah, you did. And I liked it, Miss Eaton."

Belinda wanted to tell Griffin that she liked him kissing her. But how was she going to admit that to him when supposedly he didn't appeal to her? The truth was she did like him—a little too much despite her protests.

"Have a good day, Griffin," she said instead.

"Trust me, I will," he called out.

Looking around for something she could throw at his arrogant head, Belinda realized she'd been had. Griffin hadn't kissed her because he wanted to but because he wanted to prove a point—that she was no more immune to him than the other women who chased him.

Well, he was about to get the shock of his life. She'd go along with his little game of playing house until she either tired or lost interest. And in every game there were winners and losers and Belinda Eaton didn't plan to lose.

Belinda stabbed absentmindedly at the salad with a plastic fork as she concentrated on the article in the

latest issue of *Vanity Fair.* She glanced up when she felt
the press of a body next to hers.

"What's up, Miss Ritchie?" she asked.

"That's what I should be asking you, Miss Eaton,"
said Valerie Ritchie as she slid into the chair beside
Belinda. "You didn't come in yesterday, and when I
saw a sub cover your classes this morning I was going
to call you later on tonight."

Closing the magazine, Belinda smiled at the woman
whom she'd met in graduate school. Valerie was one of
only a few teachers she befriended at one of Philadelphia's most challenging inner-city high schools. Much
of the faculty, including the administration, remained at
the school only because they were unable to find a
similar position in a better neighborhood. But she and
Valerie stayed because of the students.

"The guardianship for my sister's children was final-
ized yesterday," she said softly.

"That was fast."

"The lawyer and judge are members of the same
country club."

Valerie shook her head. "Why is it always not what
you know, but who you know?"

"That's the way of the world."

Belinda stared at Valerie, a world history and eco-
nomics teacher. Recently divorced, Valerie had
rebuffed the advances of every male teacher who'd
asked her out, claiming she wanted to wait a year
before jumping back into the dating game. The petite,
curvy natural beauty had caught the attention of the
grandson of a prominent black Philadelphia politician
who pursued her until she married him, much to the
consternation of his family, his father in particular.

Tired of the interference from her in-laws, Valerie filed for divorce and netted a sizeable settlement for her emotional pain and anguish.

"I don't envy you, Belinda."

"Why do you say that?"

"It's very noble of you to want to raise your sister's kids, especially when you have to do it alone."

A math teacher walked into the lounge and sat down on a worn leather love seat in a corner far enough away so they wouldn't be overheard. Belinda had made it a practice to keep her private and professional lives separate.

"I'm not going to raise them by myself."

Valerie gave Belinda a narrow stare. "Have you been holding out on me?"

"What are you going on about, Valerie?"

"Are you and Raymond getting married?"

Belinda shook her head. She and Dr. Raymond Miller had what she referred to as an I-95 relationship when he accepted a position as head of cardiology at an Orlando, Florida, geriatric facility. They alternated visiting each other—she visited during school recesses and Raymond whenever he could manage to take a break from the hospital.

"No."

"Why not?"

"We're just friends, Valerie."

"Do you think you'll ever stop being friends and become lovers?"

"I doubt it."

Valerie's clear brown eyes set in a flawless olive-brown face narrowed. "Are you in love with someone else?"

Belinda shook her head again. "No. Griffin and I share custody of our nieces."

"Griffin Rice," Valerie repeated loud enough for those in the room to turn and look in their direction.

Belinda angled her head closer to Valerie's. She'd just finished telling her about the arrangement she'd established with her brother-in-law when the bell rang, signaling the end of lunch. Papers, magazines and the remnants of lunch were put away as teachers left the lounge for their classrooms.

Chapter 4

"How is she getting along, Dad?" Griffin asked his father when he joined him at the picture window in the living room of the spacious apartment in Spring Garden, a neighborhood that had been completely transformed by gentrification. The nighttime view from the high-rise was spectacular.

He knew exactly what he'd look like in twenty years. An inch shy of the six-foot mark, sixty-two-year-old Lucas Rice claimed a ramrod-straight back, slender physique and a full head of shimmering silver hair. Balanced features, a cleft chin and a sensual smile drew women of all ages to him like sunflowers facing the sun. His looks and charisma posed a problem for his wives because women loved Lucas, and he in turn loved them back.

Nevertheless, Grant's death had humbled Lucas, making him aware of his own mortality. In his shared grief with Gloria and his surviving son, he'd confessed his many transgressions. It hadn't made it any easier for Griffin to hear about the number of women his father had slept with while still married to his mother, but he realized how much strength it took for Lucas to confess.

The confession signaled a turning point for everyone—especially Gloria. Surprisingly, she forgave her ex-husband, saying they'd married much too young and for the wrong reason. They'd met in college where Gloria was a library science major and Lucas was pre-med. Gloria discovered halfway through her sophomore year that she was pregnant. And instead of going to medical school, Lucas married his pregnant girlfriend and switched his major to pharmacology. Most of their marital strife was the result of Lucas not fulfilling his dream of becoming a doctor.

Lucas stole a glance at his son's profile. "She's pretty good during the day, but I found that she's a wreck at night."

Shifting slightly, Griffin turned to give Lucas an incredible stare. "What are you talking about?"

"I've been checking up on her since we…we lost Grant. We talk every day, and several nights each week we have dinner—either here, at my place, or at a restaurant. I always call her to say good-night, but that's when I lose it, son."

A slight frown furrowed Griffin's smooth forehead. "Why, Dad?"

Lucas closed his eyes, his chest rising and falling heavily. "The sound of her crying rips my heart out. I know she used to cry whenever we had an argument, but this time it's different."

"She's still grieving. We're all still grieving."

"Not like your mother, Griffin. That's why I suggested taking the cruise. I know I can't go back forty years and right all the wrongs, but I promised myself that I would spend what's left of my life making your mother happy."

"Do you love her, Dad?"

A sad smile crinkled the skin around Lucas's eyes. "I've always loved her and I will always love her."

"What about your other women?"

"There are no other women, and there hasn't been one in a long time."

Griffin chose his words carefully. "Is it because you're trying to insinuate yourself back into my mother's life?"

Lucas shook his head. "Don't worry, son. I won't hurt her."

"I'm not worried, Dad. *You* will be sorry if you hurt her again."

Lucas met Griffin's withering gaze, knowing he wasn't issuing an idle threat. He hadn't stayed to see Griffin grow to adulthood, but he was proud of how he'd turned out nevertheless. He was proud of both of his sons, and had never hesitated to give Gloria all the credit for their successes.

"Glo has been hurt enough. I'd rather walk away than cause her more pain."

Griffin smiled. It'd been a long time since he'd heard his father shorten his mother's name. Reaching into the pocket of his slacks, he took out a small envelope, slipping it into Lucas's shirt pocket. "There's enough on that gift card to buy something nice in Florence or Rome for your cabin mate."

Lucas took the envelope, staring numbly at the value

of the gift card. It was half of what he'd paid for two first-class tickets for the month-long European cruise. "I can't take this, Griffin."

"You can and you will, otherwise I'll give it to Mom, and you know she'll buy gifts for everyone but herself."

A smile flashed across the older man's face. "You're right about that. I want to bring something back for the twins. Do you have an idea of what they'd like?"

Griffin pondered his father's question for several minutes. "I believe Layla would love a Venetian *Carnevale* mask, the kind revelers wear. Sabrina likes fashion, so anything from Rome or Paris will make her very happy."

"What about Belinda?"

"What about her, Dad?"

"What do you think she'd like?"

Lucas mentioning Belinda's name quickened Griffin's pulse, as images of the kiss they'd shared came back with the force and fury of rushing rapids. He'd kissed her to see if she was actually a prude even after she'd disclosed that she was seeing someone. He hadn't believed her. He'd discovered there was indeed fire under her staid exterior. The revelation had not only shocked him, but also made him jealous of the man who was on the receiving end of Belinda Eaton's passion.

"Perfume." He'd said the first thing that came to mind because he loved the way she smelled.

"What fragrance does she wear?"

"I don't know."

"What don't you know?" asked Gloria Rice as she walked into the living room carrying a tray with dessert plates of tiny butter cookies and petits fours.

Griffin walked over and took the tray from his

mother. She looked better than she had in months, and he attributed that to the anticipation of going away for a month with the man who'd been and apparently still was the only one she'd ever loved.

In preparation for her trip, she'd had her hair cut into a close-cropped natural that showed off her delicate features and flawless chestnut-brown skin. Her dark almond-shaped eyes made her look as if she were perpetually smiling.

When she'd been informed of her son and daughter-in-law's death Gloria had stopped eating. It was only after Griffin threatened to have her force-fed that she had begun eating again, and then only small portions but enough to keep up her strength.

Now that Lucas had come back into her life, she'd managed to regain some of the weight she'd lost. When he'd asked his mother whether she was sleeping with her ex-husband, Gloria had come out with an unequivocal "no." She claimed all Lucas was good for was companionship.

"Do you know what perfume Belinda wears?"

"Yes. It's Dior's J'adore. Why do you want to know?"

"Dad's putting together a list of souvenirs he wants to bring back."

"I'm done with my list." She smiled at Lucas. "Please bring in the coffee. It should be finished brewing."

Reaching for Gloria's hand, Griffin seated her on her favorite chair. He sat on the matching ottoman, cradling her feet in his lap. "If you come back from Europe carrying my little sister or brother," he teased quietly, "I'm going to give Dad a serious beat down."

Throwing back her head, Gloria laughed until tears rolled down her face. "You don't have worry about

beating up your father because it's not going to happen."
Gloria sobered. "Speaking of children, Griffin."

"What about them, Mom?"

"I know you've adopted Grant's children, but do you
see yourself having children of your own?"

There came a long silence as he pondered her
question. "If I were to be completely honest I'd say I
don't know. Playing daddy is still too new for me to
make a decision. But I must admit I'm enjoying what
little I've experienced."

"How are you getting along with Belinda?"

"We're doing okay. It's obvious she's going to be the
stricter parent, while I'll probably let the girls do
whatever they want—except when it comes to boys. If
it were up to me they wouldn't have a boyfriend until
they graduate from high school."

Gloria shook her head. "That's unrealistic. Your
father was my first boyfriend and you see how that
ended. My granddaughters should have boys as friends
so they learn to differentiate between the good guys and
the ones who only want to sleep with them." She paused,
seemingly deep in thought. "I believe if I'd had a
daughter, Lucas wouldn't have been such a philanderer."

Griffin wanted to tell Gloria that she was wrong.
Lucas would've cheated on her if they'd had a dozen
daughters. Unfortunately, it'd taken a catastrophic
incident to bring Lucas Rice to the realization that he'd
misused and mistreated the best woman he'd ever had
and would ever hope to have. Perhaps, he mused, it
wasn't too late for his parents to start over.

Layla and Sabrina were waiting on the front porch
for Griffin when he maneuvered his SUV into the

driveway and parked behind their aunt's Volvo. They were bundled in down-filled jackets, bracing against the rapid twenty-point decline in the temperature. The past week the weather had challenged the late-March season, and won.

He smiled as he got out of his car. Maybe it was the profusion of hair flowing down and around their shoulders that made them appear older, as if they'd become young adults virtually overnight.

He wasn't disappointed when they raced off the porch to launch themselves at him. The spontaneity reminded Griffin they were still young, and as they'd done when they were children, they wanted him to catch them in midair.

"Whoa!" he cried out when he collapsed to the floor of the porch under their weight.

The front door opened and he looked up to find Belinda smiling down at him as Sabrina and Layla held him down while pinning him with what they thought were wrestling holds. Lamps flanking the door flattered her slender body in a pair of fitted jeans she'd paired with a chunky pullover. She'd also changed her hairstyle. Instead of the usual curly look it was smooth, the feathered ends curving under her chin and down around the nape of her neck.

"Do you give up?" Layla shouted, tightening her headlock.

"Yes!"

"Count him out, Aunt Lindy!" Sabrina said excitedly.

Playing along with her nieces, Belinda went to her knees and slapped the porch close to Griffin's head. "One, two, three. You're out!" The girls released Griffin, falling back and gasping in surprise when he reached for their aunt, pinning her under his body.

Burying his face against the column of her scented neck, he pressed his mouth to the silken flesh. "Come with us this weekend," he whispered near her ear.

Belinda swallowed a moan. There was no way she could ignore the hard body molded to hers, the solid pressure of bulging muscle between Griffin's thighs. She closed her eyes when a gush of moisture bathed the area between her legs.

"I... I can't." She could hardly get the words out.

"If you give her a headlock she'll give up, Uncle Griff," Layla suggested.

Griffin eased his arm under Belinda's neck. "Give up, baby," he crooned for her ears only. "Are you coming with us?" he asked loud enough for his nieces to overhear his entreaty.

"No-o-o-o!"

Sabrina went to her knees. "Please, Aunt Lindy. Please come with us. Uncle Griff said we were going to have a movie night."

"Pul-eeese," Layla moaned melodramatically.

Belinda closed her eyes. *Oh no!* a silent voice shouted when Griffin ground his groin against hers. She couldn't believe what he was doing to her—in front of their nieces no less. If she didn't stop him, then she was going to embarrass herself. Her long-celibate body indicated that she was on the brink of climaxing.

"Okay. I'll go."

"Pinky swear?" Griffin asked, grinning triumphantly.

She nodded. "Yes. Pinky swear."

Layla and Sabrina exchanged high fives as they turned to go back into the house to retrieve their overnight bags. They'd spent most of the afternoon exchanging text messages with their uncle to enlist his help in getting their aunt to join them for the weekend after she revealed she hadn't planned to do anything but read and watch DVDs.

As soon as the door banged behind them, Belinda said between clenched teeth, "Get the hell off me!"

Griffin eased up, but not enough for Belinda to escape. He didn't want to stand up until his erection went down. He hadn't expected his body to betray him, nor had he expected Belinda's response.

"Watch your language, baby. You don't want *our* children to grow up using foul language."

"They've heard worse," she said flippantly, "and no doubt from their classmates."

"I know you hear it at the high school, but I'd prefer that Sabrina and Layla not hear it at home."

Belinda affected a facetious smile. "Please let me up, Griffin."

He smiled. "That's better, darling."

Waiting until Griffin moved off her and helped her to her feet, Belinda caught the front of his sweatshirt. Standing on tiptoe, she thrust her face close to his. "If you ever hump me in front of the girls again I'll hurt you, Griffin Rice."

Griffin winked at her. "Would you prefer that I hump you in private? I know I don't appeal to you, but your body is saying something else."

Her fist tightened. "What exactly is my body saying?"

"That regardless of how we may feel about each other, our bodies are in agreement." He leaned in closer. "I could smell sex coming from your pores."

Belinda let her hand fall at the same time her jaw dropped. "How dare you! Your arrogance just supplanted whatever common sense—"

"Cut the act, Belinda!" Griffin said angrily, cutting off her tirade. "It's only a normal reaction between a man and woman, so don't confuse sex and desire with love. I'm not in love with you, and I doubt whether you'll ever be in love with me. Circumstances beyond our control have forced us into a situation we never would've or could've imagined. I didn't ask to be a father but I intend to make the best of it, and if that means making sacrifices to keep my vow to my dead brother then I will."

"Pray tell, Griffin, just what are you sacrificing?"

The seconds ticked off as he stared at the woman who intrigued him more than he wanted. The sexy godmother who made him want her when everything said that she was so wrong for him.

"Having a normal relationship with a woman."

"Don't you mean sleeping with other women?"

"That, too."

"My heart bleeds for you, Griffin. If you think I'm going to become a replacement for your *other* women, then think again, mister. I don't play house."

His eyebrows flickered. "Do you play at all?"

"Yes," she retorted. "What I do play is for keeps."

"If you play for keeps, then where is your so-called boyfriend?"

Oh, you're trying to be slick and get into my business, Belinda mused. "You'll get to meet Raymond when he comes up from Florida this summer."

"Why do I have to wait for the summer?"

"That's when he'll be able to get away."

"Don't you mean that's when he'll be paroled?"

"Oh, no you didn't!"

"Yes, I did, Belinda. Is your Raymond in a Florida

jail? I'm asking because I don't want that type of element around my daughters."

"Why are they always *your* daughters, Griffin?" Belinda shot back, the timbre of her voice escalating along with her temper. "Aren't they also my children?"

"I thought we now belong to both of you."

Belinda and Griffin spun around. They hadn't heard Sabrina when she'd come out of the house. They were so busy going at each other that they hadn't realized they weren't alone.

Belinda went over to hug her. "Of course you belong to both of us. You and Layla are my daughters."

"What about Uncle Griff?"

"You're his daughter, too."

"If that's true, then why were you fighting?"

"We weren't fighting, sweetheart."

"It sounded to me as if you were fighting."

Belinda met Griffin's knowing gaze over Sabrina's head. As new parents they'd made an unforgivable faux pas—argue in front of their children. "There're times when adults don't agree with something, so it may sound as if we're arguing. Your uncle and I love you and your sister. We made a promise to take care of you and make certain you're safe. I'm going to ask you and Layla to be patient with us because we're newbies playing mom and dad."

Sabrina smiled. "You already sound like a mom even though Uncle Griff needs more practice at being a daddy."

"Well, excuse me," Griffin drawled. "What do I have to do to sound like a daddy?"

"First of all you have to learn to say *'that's enough, young lady.'*"

Griffin forced back a smile. He'd lost count of the

number of times Grant had issued his favorite warning. "What else?"

Sabrina narrowed her gaze. "There's *'did you do what your mother told you to do?'*"

Belinda pressed her palms together. "I like that one."

"You would," Griffin mumbled under his breath.

Layla, carrying a large quilted tote, joined them on the porch, frowning. "Aunt Lindy, I thought you were coming with us."

"I am. I just have to put a few things in a bag. Don't leave without me."

"We won't," came three voices.

Chapter 5

Proper attire for movie night in Paoli was pajamas and fuzzy slippers. Belinda, her head supported on a mound of overstuffed pillows, lay on the carpeted floor beside Griffin, while Layla and Sabrina were huddled together, sharing a large throw pillow. They were watching *Akeelah and the Bee* for the umpteenth time. The film had become a favorite of the twins, along with most of the feature-length animated films from Disney/Pixar. Sabrina, who'd demonstrated promise as a budding artist, had expressed interest in becoming an animator.

It was only Belinda's second trip to Griffin's house, and there were a few changes since her last visit more than five years before. He'd added an in-ground pool, expanded the outdoor patio to include a kitchen and added another room at the rear of the house that served as a home office. File folders bulging with contracts, strewn over a workstation, were a testament to a less-than-efficient filing system.

Griffin made a big production of preparing for movie night when he taught the girls how to build a fire in the fireplace. Refreshments included popcorn, s'mores, bonbons and cherry Twizzlers.

"Who wins the bee?" Griffin whispered to Belinda.

Layla sat up. "Don't tell him, Aunt Lindy!"

Belinda tickled Griffin's ribs through his T-shirt. "I'm not telling."

Griffin caught her fingers. "Don't do that."

"Are you ticklish?"

Not releasing her hand, he stared at Belinda for a full minute before lacing their fingers together. "Yes."

Smiling, she winked at him. "Do you have any other weaknesses I should know about?"

Griffin closed his eyes rather than let Belinda see how much she affected him, how much she'd changed him and his life in less than a few weeks. How could he tell her that he liked her because she was different from the other women he'd been involved with, that he wanted what she gave Raymond—her Sunshine State lover—and like Belinda, if he had to play then he wanted it to be for keeps? Spending a Friday night at home watching movies with Belinda and the girls was the highlight of his week—and something he could very easily get used to.

"That's it," he lied smoothly, redirecting his attention to the large plasma screen mounted on the wall. Griffin pretended interest in the movie when it was the woman pressed to his side that he found so intriguing.

* * *

Belinda had just dozed off when she heard the soft knock on the door. Sitting up, she turned on the bedside lamp. "Who is it?"

"It's Count Dracula, and I've come to suck your blood," a deep voice crooned in a perfect Romanian dialect.

Belinda smiled. "Sorry, count, but I'm all out of blood."

"Curses!" he snarled, this time sounding like a pirate.

"Come in, Griffin." The door opened and Griffin walked in, wearing a pair of black pajama pants and matching T-shirt.

Friday night at the movies had not only been enjoyable but also enlightening. She had seen another side to Griffin's personality, the opposite of the aggressive and competitive attorney who'd become notorious for holding out until he got the best deal for his clients. He had a really wicked sense of humor, telling jokes and deliberately flubbing the punch lines. Sabrina and Layla had adored the attention he lavished on them and they, in turn, reciprocated in kind.

"Is movie night over?" She'd found herself dozing off and on until she decided it was time to go to bed, leaving before the end of the film.

Griffin nodded. "When I told the girls they had to brush their teeth before turning in, they said I sounded like Aunt Lindy."

"Is that a good thing?" she teased, smiling.

"I'd say it is."

"What are you doing?" she shrieked when he ran and jumped onto the bed, flopping down on the mattress and pressing his back to the headboard.

Crossing his bare feet at the ankles, Griffin gave Belinda a sidelong glance. "I came to talk." Before settling down to watch the movie, he'd watched as she brushed and pinned Layla's and Sabrina's freshly relaxed hair, covering theirs with bandannas before doing her own. Her smooth transition from aunt to surrogate mother was nothing short of amazing.

"What's so urgent that you can't wait until tomorrow?"

"What do you think about getting the girls a dog?"

Belinda went completely still. "What kind of dog, Griffin?"

"Don't worry, Belinda, it won't be a pit bull or Rottweiler."

"What kind of dog?" she asked again.

"A Yorkshire terrier. One of my neighbors has a purebred bitch that whelped a litter of pups about three months ago. She's sold off all but two, and I told her that I would have to talk to you before offering to buy one."

"A puppy," she whispered. "You want me to take care of a puppy?"

"Sabrina and Layla will take care of it."

"I don't think so, Griffin. You're fooling yourself if you believe girls their age are going to take care of a dog. I'll wind up feeding, bathing and walking it. And what's going to happen when it gnaws on my rugs and furniture?"

Griffin dropped an arm over Belinda's shoulders, bringing her cheek to his chest. "You've got it all wrong."

"No, I don't."

"Please don't say no until you see them. They're adorable."

"I'm certain they're adorable but—"

"Baby, please," he crooned softly. "Grant promised the girls they could have a dog."

Tilting her head, Belinda stared at Griffin looking down at her. The soft glow from the lamp flattered the contours of his lean face. "Donna didn't say anything to me about getting a dog."

"Grant wanted to surprise them. I'll buy the cage, wee-wee pads, food and chew toys. I'll also commit to covering the vet and grooming expenses, and of course the pooch will need one of those designer puppy carriers that cost an arm and two legs."

She smiled. "Why does it sound as if you're running a con on me?"

He returned her smile. "I didn't mean for it—"

"It's okay," she said, cutting him off. "When are we going to look at the puppies?"

Griffin kissed her forehead. "Tomorrow after breakfast."

"I must have *sucker* written on my forehead."

He laughed softly, the warm sound rumbling in his chest. "Why should you be any different from me?"

"Are we really soft, Griffin?"

"No. We're just two people who want the best for the children we've been entrusted to love and protect."

"You're right," Belinda said after a pregnant pause. "I always believed I'd grow up to fall in love, marry and have children of my own. Never in my wildest dreams would I have thought that I'd be raising my sister's children. What makes it so challenging is that they're not little kids, but pre-teens who're beginning to assert their independence. I try and do the best I can, but what frightens me is what will I do or say if, or when, they come out with *'you can't tell me what to do because you're not my mother.'*"

"Let's hope it never happens, but if it does then I'll step in."

Belinda tried to sit up, but was thwarted when Griffin held her fast. "You're not going to hit them."

He frowned at her. "I'd never hit a child. What I can assure you is that my bark is a great deal louder than yours."

"I'll not have you yelling at them."

"What's it going to be, Belinda? You can't have it both ways. There's going to come a time when they're going to challenge you, because all kids do it. But the dilemma for us will be how do we deal with it as parents. And if I have to raise my voice to get them off your back, then I will. Remember, they're twins, so they're apt to tag-team you."

Belinda remembered when Donna broke curfew and Roberta was sitting in the living room waiting up for her. Donna said something flippant and all Belinda remembered was Roberta telling Donna that she'd brought her into the world and she could also take her out. Her mother's tirade woke up the entire household and it took all of Dwight Eaton's gentle persuasion to defuse the situation.

It was after the volatile confrontation that Belinda made a promise to herself: if and when she had children she would never scream at them, because not only was punishment more effective, but also the results lasted longer.

"If you're going to raise your voice, then I don't want to be anywhere around," she told Griffin.

"Dammit, Belinda, you act like I'm going to verbally abuse them. When it comes to discipline we are going to have to be on the same page, or else they're going to play one off the other."

"I know," she whispered, burying her face between his neck and shoulder.

"What do you do when your students act out?"

"I put them out of my class, and then write them up."

"Do you have problems with the boys?"

"What kind of problems?"

"Do they try and come on to you?"

"A few have tried, but when I give them a 'screw face' then they usually back off."

"Show me a 'screw face.'" Easing out of Griffin's comforting embrace, Belinda sat up and glared at him. There *was* something in Belinda's gaze that was frightening. "How do you do that?" he asked.

She smiled. "Practice, practice, practice. I have more problems with my female students than the males. Some of them outweigh me, so they believe they can take me out with very little effort. In not so many words, I tell them I can roll with the best of them."

"You're not talking about fighting a student?"

"Of course not. But what they don't know is that I have a black belt in tae kwon do, with distinction in sparring and power breaking. Myles studied karate for years, earned his black belt, but didn't like competing. I, on the other hand, loved competitions."

"Do you still compete?"

"No. It's been a long time since my last competition. A lot of teachers refuse to teach in rough neighborhoods, but the confidence I gained from a decade of martial arts training and the fact that these kids need dedicated teachers is why I stay."

"So you can kick my butt."

Belinda smiled. "With one arm tied behind my back," she said, teasingly.

"Ouch!" he kidded, pressing her back to the mattress.

"When I first met you I thought you were cute and I wanted to ask you out, but you were Miss Attitude personified."

"I was nineteen and you had already graduated law school, so I thought you were too old for me."

"I'm only five years older than you. I graduated high school at sixteen, college at twenty and law school at twenty-three. That made me an accelerated student, not an older man."

"You seemed so much older then."

"What about now?"

"When I saw you rolling around on the porch with Layla and Sabrina I had serious doubts as to your maturity."

"They love it when I wrestle with them," Griffin drawled. "Fast-forward thirteen years, and I'm going to ask you something I should've asked when you were nineteen. Belinda Eaton, will you go out with me?"

"You're kidding, aren't you?"

"Why do you think I'm kidding?"

"Not only are we aunt, uncle and godparents but our nieces' legal guardians. We sleep in each other's homes, you have a key to mine and I to yours, but right now we're in bed together. Dating would be ludicrous given our situation."

"You're right about us sharing a situation."

"Is there something wrong with that, Griffin?"

"There's nothing wrong with it, but I would prefer having a relationship with you aside from what we share with Sabrina and Layla. That way I could get to know you better."

Belinda was strangely flattered by Griffin's interest in her. She experienced a gamut of emotions that didn't let her think clearly. Circumstances beyond their control had brought them together and the man whom she'd come to believe couldn't be faithful to one woman wanted a relationship with her.

"I'll have to think about it."

His expressive eyebrows lifted. "What's there to think about?"

Belinda gave him a long, penetrating stare. "I have to decide whether I'm willing to see you exclusively."

"Does that mean you'll give up Sunshine?"

"Who's Sunshine?"

"Your pen-pal chump living off the taxpayers in a Sunshine State prison."

"Raymond is not a chump," she said in defense of the kindest man whom she had the pleasure of knowing.

"He's in Florida and you're in Pennsylvania, which means you live at least a thousand miles apart. How often do you see him, Belinda? Or better yet—how many times a year, if he's not incarcerated, does he make love to you? How do you know if he's being faithful to you?"

Her temper flared as she sat up. "How do I know you'll be faithful to me?"

"You don't. All you'll have is my word."

Belinda wanted to tell Griffin that she was beginning to like him, in fact, like him a little too much to be indifferent to his sexual magnetism. When he'd held her down on the porch she'd been on the verge of climaxing and that just looking at him made her body hot and throb with a need long denied. Griffin was right about Raymond. She didn't know whether he was sleeping with another woman but that wasn't her concern because he was her friend. She'd fallen in love only once in her life, and it ended with her moving off campus to come back home. It took years before she trusted a man enough to sleep with him.

"If I can't have Sunshine, then it definitely has to be no skanks, 'chicken heads' or hoochies for you."

Throwing back his head, Griffin laughed. "You drive a hard bargain, Lindy Eaton."

"It has to be all or nothing."

Griffin ran a forefinger down the length of her nose. "If you ever have to negotiate a deal always remember to give your competitor an out."

"Is that how you see me, Griffin? Am I a competitor or an opponent?"

"Neither."

"Then what am I?"

"I'm someone who's concerned about you. You'd fallen asleep less than half an hour into the movie. I know you're exhausted. You no longer cook, clean, wash and iron for one, but three. Layla told me you spent more than an hour folding laundry."

A scowl settled into Belinda's features. "You have the girls spying on me?"

"No, Belinda. I only asked them how their week went and both were only too willing to tell me. The reason I want to take you out is to give you a break. It can be one night a week. We can leave Layla and Sabrina at your parents' or with my mother when she comes back. You can let me know in advance what you want to do or where you'd like to eat and I'll make it happen."

Belinda's expression brightened. "If all you want to do is to take me out to dinner, then that means that I don't have to give up Raymond."

"It doesn't matter because I get to see his woman a lot more than he does."

The slow, sexy smile that never failed to make women sit up and take notice of Griffin Rice spread over his face as he moved over Belinda, supporting his weight on his elbows.

Belinda's breasts felt heavy, her nipples swelling as she leaned into the solid wall of his chest. For years she'd watched Griffin with other women, wondering why, other than his gorgeous face, they chased him and now she knew. He was inherently masculine *and* sexy, and it didn't matter that she was another in a long line of women who would get to sample what the celebrity lawyer was offering. She opened her mouth to his kiss, drowning in the sexual heat, succumbing to the sensual spell that made her feel as if she and the man holding her to his heart were the last two people on earth.

Griffin's heart slammed against his ribs when he showered kisses around Belinda's lips and along her jaw. Lowering his head, he fastened his mouth along the column of her velvety, scented neck, nipping, suckling, licking her as if she were a frothy confection.

"You taste and smell so good," he mumbled over and over.

Baring her throat, Belinda closed her eyes. She wanted to tell Griffin that he felt and smelled good, too, but the words were locked in her throat when a longing she'd never known seized her mind and body, refusing to let her go.

Without warning the spell shattered when his hands moved under her pajama top and cupped her breasts. "Griffin, no! We can't!"

"I know, baby," he gasped near her ear. He couldn't make love to Belinda while the girls were in the house, and not when he couldn't protect her against an unplanned pregnancy.

Her breathing coming in uneven pants, Belinda moaned softly. "Go to bed, Griffin."

He smiled. "I'm already in bed."

"*Your* bed," she ordered softly. "Good night, Griffin."

Burying his face between Belinda's breasts, Griffin closed his eyes. He didn't want to let her go, but he had to. Reluctantly, he moved off the bed. "Good night, Belinda."

It took a long time after Griffin left her bedroom for Belinda to fall asleep. The thrumming in the lower part of her body had become a reminder of what she'd missed and needed.

Chapter 6

"I'll take both of them."

Belinda turned on her heel, walking out of the room to wait on the Sandersons' back porch. She had to get away from Griffin or say something she would regret for the rest of her life.

Griffin had called his neighbor and set up an appointment to see the puppies. He'd told his nieces that they were going shopping after eating out at a local diner. But they were totally unaware that *going shopping* meant looking for a dog.

The remaining three-month-old Yorkies, both males, were spirited, friendly *and* adorable. The only question was which one Sabrina and Layla would choose. Belinda realized the quandary when each girl picked up a puppy, cradled it to her chest and then refused to relinquish them when Griffin told them to pick one. He'd become a victim of his own negotiating skills when each girl pleaded her case as to why they didn't want to share one dog.

"I think your wife is a little upset," Nicole Sanderson said in a quiet voice to Griffin. "Why don't you go and see what's wrong."

Nicole was pleasantly surprised when Griffin Rice followed through on his promise to set up an appointment to look at the puppies. She, however, was more than surprised when he revealed that he was also coming with his wife and daughters. Paoli was a small town, with a population of fifty-four hundred, and it was inevitable that most residents' paths would occasionally cross in the friendly, close-knit community. When Griffin Rice purchased a home in Paoli nearly eight years before, the town's grapevine hummed with the news that they had a celebrity living among them.

"I'll be right back," Griffin said to the woman who was looking forward to selling her last two purebred Yorkshire terriers. Opening the door, he saw Belinda with her back to him.

"Lindy, baby."

"Don't you *dare* say a mumbling word to me, Griffin Rice!" With wide eyes, she rounded on him. "Don't call me Lindy, and I'm not your *baby.*"

Griffin didn't understand what'd set her off. She'd agreed to their nieces having a dog, so what could be so wrong with them having one more? "What's wrong?"

"What's wrong?" Belinda repeated, approaching him. When she closed her eyes the tips of her lashes touched her cheekbones, and when they opened again the dark orbs were awash with moisture. "Marriages fail because couples don't communicate. They argue about money, child rearing and lack of affection but not necessarily in that order. We are *not* communicating, Griffin, and we aren't even married. I agreed to one puppy. How on earth did it become two?"

Griffin resisted the urge to pull Belinda in his arms. "Didn't you hear what Layla and Sabrina said? They said this is the first time in their lives they're not treated as if they're joined at the hip. You're the only one who doesn't refer to them as *the twins,* or who bought them matching outfits. They had to wait twelve years to get their own rooms, where they won't grow up as copies of each other. You relate to them as freethinkers, individuals, and that's what they've become. Sabrina doesn't want to share her puppy with Layla and vice versa."

"Two puppies translate into twice the mess."

Taking a step, Griffin rested a hand on the nape of Belinda's neck. "A mess you won't have to deal with. Each girl will be responsible for her own puppy. Not having to share will eliminate arguments as to whose week it is to clean the crate."

Belinda tried ignoring the subtle, seductive fragrance of Griffin's aftershave—but failed. "Why do you insist on complicating my life?"

"How am I doing that?"

"Instead of looking after one puppy when *our daughters* are away on their class trip, I'll have to look after two."

Griffin brushed a light kiss over her parted lips. "Remember, Lindy, you're not in this alone. I'll help you."

"When? Don't you have a company to run?"

He nodded. "A business I'm currently downsizing from six to two. I've already begun moving files from the Philly office to Paoli. I'm putting my marketing manager on retainer, and I expect to hire a retired para-

legal who wants to come on board part-time, which fits
perfectly into my business strategy. She'll be responsible for typing contracts and filing court documents."

"You're moving your office." The question was a
statement.

"Yes. That's why I built the addition onto the house.
To be honest, I should've done it years ago. The money
I've spent renting a suite of offices in downtown Philly
could've fed every child in a small African country for
at least a year."

"Where are you going to conduct your meetings?"

"In whatever city the team owners' call home. If it's
local, then I'll reserve a room at a restaurant with good
food and service, or a hotel suite."

The seconds ticked off as Belinda and Griffin stared
at each other. He hadn't shaved, and the stubble on his
lean jaw enhanced rather than detracted from his classic
good looks. Dressed in an olive-green barn jacket, jeans,
black crewneck sweater and matching low-heeled
leather boots he reminded her of a Ralph Lauren ad.

"When did you decide all this?" she asked, breaking
the silence.

"It was the day I went to clean out Grant's office—
something I'd avoided doing for weeks—because I
didn't want to admit to myself that my brother had been
right when he said that the price of success is grossly
overrated.

"As I stood in his twentieth-floor corner office overlooking downtown Philadelphia I could hear a voice in
my head. At first I thought it was my imagination, but
it wasn't because I was reliving the one time I saw my
brother drunk. He'd just gotten a promotion and a
coveted corner office. I'll never forget his face when he

stared at me, then said, *'Success don't mean shit when you look at what you have to sacrifice in order to achieve it.'* At first I thought he was just being maudlin until he talked about how he was able to remember everything about his clients' stock portfolios but he couldn't remember his wife's birthday or their wedding anniversary. He talked about the meetings and business trips that took him away from home where invariably he'd miss a recital or his daughters' school plays. For Grant, making it had become all-consuming. I suppose it had something to do with proving to your parents that Donna hadn't made a mistake when she agreed to marry him."

"My parents were never against your brother marrying my sister," Belinda said, defensively.

"I didn't understand how Grant felt until I met your family for the first time. My first impression was that the Eatons were snobs. You come from generations of teachers, doctors and lawyers, while my mother and father were the first in their family to graduate from college. Grant had less than a month before he would get his degree and he still hadn't heard from any of his prospective employers when your father took him aside and said that if he ever needed money to take care of his daughter or grandchildren then he shouldn't hesitate to come to him. His offer cut Grant to the quick, but he smiled at Dr. Eaton and said that he wouldn't have married his daughter if he hadn't been able to support her.

"So, the day Grant got his seven-figure salary and all the perks that went along with his position, he warned me about putting success before family. I never wanted children because I didn't want them growing up with parents who fought more than they made love. And since life doesn't always play out the way we want it to, I'm committed to making the best of the hand I've been dealt. I promised my brother I would take care of his children in the event anything happened to him, and that means being available for parent-teacher conferences, school concerts, supervising sleep-overs and chauffeuring them when it's time for college tours."

Belinda tried to hide her confusion. She'd believed that Grant worked long hours so that Donna could be a stay-at-home mother and the envy of the other women in their social circle who were jealous because they were working mothers.

"I didn't know," she said softly when she recovered her voice.

"I doubt if Donna knew how Grant felt. He wasn't one for opening up about himself—not even to his wife. In that way he's a lot like my dad. It has taken my father more than forty years to tell my mother that he'd been carrying around a world of resentment because she got pregnant and he had to drop out of medical school to take care of her and their child."

Belinda couldn't stop the frown forming between her eyes. "He should've accepted half the blame. After all, she couldn't get pregnant by herself, Griffin."

"You're preaching to the choir, beautiful. People always blame others when something goes wrong in their life because it's easier than accepting responsibility that perhaps they, too, were wrong."

Belinda lowered her gaze, staring at Griffin's strong, brown throat. "I should apologize to you."

"For what?"

"I retract what I said about you not having any redeeming qualities."

"You said no such thing." Belinda's head came up, her exotic-looking eyes filling with confusion. "You said, and I quote, *'I'm not attracted to you, and there's nothing about you that I find even remotely appealing.'*" He placed his free hand over his heart. "You have no idea of how much you hurt me when you said that."

Belinda was hard-pressed not to laugh at his affected theatrics. "Suck it up, Rice. What I said pales in comparison to when you said I wasn't at the top of your list for what you'd want in a woman."

Griffin angled his head and smiled. "Guess what?"

"What?"

"I lied."

Her smile matched his. "I suppose since we're into true confessions, then I'll admit that I lied, too." She wanted to tell Griffin that she was attracted to him and found him *very* appealing.

Griffin brushed a light kiss over her parted lips. "Let's go back inside and close this deal. I'm certain Sabrina and Layla are anxious to take their puppies home."

Belinda caught the sleeve of Griffin's jacket. "Before we go in I just want to remind you that the girls are leaving to go on a class trip to D.C. two days before I'm out for spring break. We're going to have to make arrangements to board the puppies for those days."

"They won't have to go to a kennel."

"They're too young to be left alone."

"Don't worry so much, Lindy. I'll stay at your place until you come home."

"What if you have to leave town on business?"

"Whatever it is can wait," he said softly. "Remember, family comes first, even if it's of the four-legged furry persuasion."

* * *

Roberta Eaton smiled at her granddaughters, each holding a tiny puppy with dark fur and tan markings. "What do we have here?"

"Grams, this is Cecil Rice," Sabrina announced in a loud, dramatic voice. "He's a Yorkshire terrier."

"And this is Nigel Rice," Layla said, introducing her puppy. "We gave them British names because Aunt Lindy told us that Yorkshire is in England."

Roberta Eaton pressed her palms together. "They're so tiny. How much do they weigh?"

"Nigel is two pounds and three ounces and Cecil two pounds and six ounces," Sabrina answered, bragging like a proud mother.

Roberta shook her head in amazement. "Together they don't even weigh five pounds." She leaned over, kissing her granddaughters who were now as tall as she was. "Go show your Gramps the puppies, then put them away because it's time to eat."

Belinda hugged and kissed her mother before heading toward the kitchen. She hadn't missed sharing a Sunday dinner with her parents since Donna passed away because she knew what it meant to her mother to have at least one of her children with her for what throughout past generations had become a family day.

Myles, who lived and worked in Pittsburgh, wasn't expected to return until the end of the school year, and her younger sister, Chandra, was now a Peace Corps worker assigned to teaching young children in Bahia.

Roberta gestured to the tall, casually dressed man standing behind her daughter, clutching the handle of a crate. "Griffin, please find some place to put that doggy prison, and then come eat."

Griffin complied, putting the wire crate in a corner of the spacious entryway. "I have to go back to the car and bring in dessert."

"You didn't have to bring anything. I made a coconut cake."

Smiling and sharing a knowing look with Belinda, Griffin said, "I guess ours will keep."

"No doubt," Belinda crooned, playing along with him.

Roberta caught the surreptitious exchange between her daughter and Griffin. "What did you bring?"

"Carrot cake."

"From where, Griffin?"

"Ms. Tootsie's Soul Food Cafe."

"Bertie, stop playing," Dwight Eaton called out with his approach. "You know you love Ms. Tootsie's carrot cake. But then again, any dessert from Ms. Tootsie's isn't as good as yours," he added quickly, always the diplomat.

Belinda gave her father a wide grin. He always said the right thing. Dr. Dwight Eaton was only a couple of inches taller than his wife, but what he lacked in height he compensated for with wit and personality. His patients loved him as much for his medical expertise as his gentle bedside manner. His dark brown face was smooth, except for a few lines around his equally dark eyes behind a pair of rimless glasses.

"How are you, Lindy?"

"Wonderful, Daddy."

Dwight smiled at Griffin. "Are you taking good care of my girls?"

"I'm doing the best I can, sir."

The older man waved a hand. "Please, Griffin, none of that 'sir' business. Don't forget you're family."

Voices raised in excitement preceded a streak of dark

fur running across the living room. Roberta caught a puppy—Belinda still couldn't distinguish whether he was Nigel or Cecil because their markings were identical—and Griffin put the runaway puppy into the crate, while she went to retrieve the cake from his SUV.

A quarter of an hour later, everyone sat down at the dining room table to enjoy a traditional Southern dinner of macaroni and cheese, smothered pork chops, collard greens, buttery corn bread and sweet tea.

Sabrina and Layla talked nonstop about school, the students who rode the bus with them on their new route and the research they'd gathered from the Internet on Yorkies. It was the first Sunday dinner since the death of their parents that the sisters were animated and their mood ebullient. Both decided to forego dessert to play with the whining, yipping puppies that were anxious to be released from their confinement.

Griffin, at Belinda's urging, said their goodbyes at six to return home and prepare for the upcoming week. When Belinda retired for bed later that night her thoughts were of Griffin—how she'd come to look forward to seeing him, sharing meals and the responsibility of raising their nieces.

Belinda stared at her reflection in the mirror, not recognizing the image. It wasn't so much that her face had changed but the woman to whom the face belonged—*she* had changed.

She never would've imagined four months ago, or even four weeks ago that she would've accepted Griffin Rice's request to step into the role as his hostess. She'd rehearsed for the part by making his house appear lived in. With the exception of his home office, every room in the large colonial was picture perfect, as if each piece of furniture and objet d'art had been selected and positioned for a magazine layout.

Griffin admitted to hiring a design firm to decorate his house in a style reminiscent of grand Caribbean plantation homes erected during the British colonial period. Dark, heavy mahogany four-poster beds with posts engraved with decorative pineapples, leaves and vines, tables with curving legs, highboys, armoires, secretaries, settees, wall mirrors and chests of drawers transported you back to an era of ruling-class elegance whose enormous wealth was derived from slaves, sugar and rum.

It'd taken her less than a day to transform the house into a home with large green plants in glazed hand-painted vases, fresh flowers and dozens of pillars, votives and tea lights in decorative holders. The gathering was small, with a confirmed guest list of fourteen. A caterer and bartender arrived an hour before the first guests were scheduled to arrive.

For the first time in a week, anticipation at meeting their sports idol shifted Layla's and Sabrina's attention from their pets to the party. Much to Belinda's surprise, the girls kept their promise to take care of the puppies. They set their clocks to rise earlier than usual to clean the cage and put out food and clean water for Cecil and Nigel before readying themselves for school. Playing with the puppies had become a priority. As soon as they came home after school the cage was opened and each puppy bounded out to pounce on its respective owner.

She'd continued to call the Yorkies by the wrong name until Griffin pointed out that Nigel had a tiny tan spot on the tip of his tail. The dilemma of transporting the puppies and their supplies between households was eliminated when Griffin bought a cage large enough to accommodate both pups and purchased an ample supply of wee-wee pads, food, treats and chew toys to have on hand in Paoli.

Peering closer in the mirror, she checked her makeup for the last time, pleased with the results. Eye shadow, which she rarely wore, and vibrant vermilion lipstick highlighted her eyes and lips. And, because the get-together was casual, Belinda had chosen a pair of black stretch cuffed capris, a long-sleeved, off-the-shoulder fitted top and added an additional three inches to her five-six height with peep-toe pumps.

She left the bedroom and walked down the hallway to the staircase, shiny curls bouncing around her head and face with each step. After a week of painstakingly brushing her hair each night to keep the strands smooth, she'd gone back to her curly hairstyle.

Her steps slowed as she looked down to find Griffin waiting for her at the bottom of the staircase. Belinda smiled. She and Griffin were dressed alike. He was wearing a black pullover, slacks and slip-ons. The recessed light glinted off his close-cropped black hair.

Griffin extended his hand, helping Belinda as she stepped off the last step. His gaze lingered on the curls framing her round face, then moved lower to her full mouth outlined in a shimmering, sexy red shade. However, it was her eyes, the lids darkened, lashes spiked and lengthened by mascara that held him enthralled. Expertly applied makeup had served to highlight and accentuate Belinda Eaton's natural beauty.

He hadn't lied to Belinda when he told her that he'd dated his share of women, although he was very discriminating with whom he slept. But none of them could match her natural beauty.

"You look so incredibly beautiful." The sincerity in his compliment was evident.

Lowering her gaze, Belinda glanced up at him through her lashes. "Thank you."

He angled his head and pressed a kiss to her ear. "You're welcome." He didn't think he would ever get used to her smell. It was an aphrodisiac he was helpless to resist.

It'd taken Griffin only two weeks to come to the realization that he *did* like his nieces' surrogate mother, that he'd changed his opinion of her and he wanted to get closer to the intelligent, intriguing woman who unknowingly made him forget all the others.

Increasing his protective hold, he tucked her hand into the bend of his elbow and led her across the living room. Recorded music floated from concealed speakers throughout the first floor. An outdoor fireplace provided additional warmth for those who wanted to dine or sit outdoors.

"I asked Keith to get here earlier than the others. That way Sabrina and Layla can talk to him one on one."

Belinda smiled. "I'm willing to bet they'll do more gawking than talking."

"You're probably right." Reaching into a pocket of his slacks, he took out an ultra-thin digital camera. "Evidence," he drawled, grinning. "I'm certain they're going to want to prove to their friends that they *do* know Keith Ennis."

"I hope it doesn't backfire on them."

Griffin's expression mirrored confusion. "Why would you say that?"

"If they tell everyone their uncle's on a first-name basis with a major league ballplayer, some students can get jealous. I've seen it happen enough at my school with a few situations escalating into bullying and fighting."

"I've seen that happen, too, but thankfully most are good kids."

"Speaking of good—you know the girls adore you, Griffin."

He lifted his eyebrows. "They don't adore me any more than they love you, Belinda. I'm sure they see me as Santa or a magic genie that grants their wishes. It's you who must deal with them twenty-four-seven, but instead of withering they've bloomed. I know they miss their mom and dad, but you've saved them."

Belinda didn't know why, but she felt as if she was holding her breath and waiting for the time when one or both of the twins would experience a meltdown. "You have to remember that they were in therapy only days after we buried Donna and Grant," she reminded Griffin. "I don't want to think of what would've happened to them if they hadn't had professional help."

Griffin shook his head. "Therapy aside, it's you and how you relate to them that makes the difference. I overheard them talking about how much they love mani-pedies—whatever that is—and getting their hair done every week."

"A mani-pedi is a manicure and pedicure. I go every week, so I just take them along with me."

"Stop trying to minimize your importance in their lives, Belinda," Griffin chided softly. "You're not Donna, but she knew what she was doing when she asked you to take care of her children. In other words, Belinda Eaton, you are an incredible mother, and I hope Mr. Sunshine knows how lucky he is to have someone like you."

Belinda was caught off guard by the warmth in

Griffin's voice and wanted to tell him that he didn't have to concern himself with Raymond Miller. "I need to tell you—" The chiming of the doorbell preempted what she was going to tell Griffin about the man who was her friend and not her lover.

Griffin pressed his face to Belinda's soft, sweet-smelling hair. "I'll be right back."

She stood in the middle of the living room staring at the massive floral arrangement on an antique English pedestal table until delicious wafting aromas coming from the kitchen propelled her into action, and she turned and made her way toward the rear of the house.

The night before, Sabrina had admitted that she liked staying over in her uncle's house because it made her feel as if she'd stepped back in time. What the teenager liked in particular was that although Griffin had enclosed the back porch, it was still accessible through the French doors. When the doors were open the space was perfect for dining al fresco. Belinda viewed it as the perfect place for having tea or simply enjoying the landscape while rocking on the porch.

She stopped at the entrance to the kitchen. A toque-wearing chef, wielding a whisk with a vengeance in a large sauté pan, ordered a waiter to bring him a platter. "Today, please!" he drawled impatiently.

Leaving as quickly and quietly as she'd entered, Belinda reversed course, passing the dining room where the bartender was setting up. Griffin had decided on buffet-style service because it was more in keeping with the casualness of the gathering. His invitations stressed casual attire, and anyone wearing a tie or suit would be ushered out the door.

Grant and Donna had been frequent guests at the

social gatherings Griffin hosted at his house, but Belinda always had responded by politely declining. At first the invitations slowed in frequency then they stopped entirely. Donna always called to tell her who she'd met, or brag about the quality of the food, then ended the conversation with *"You don't know what you were missing."* Belinda's rejoinder was always, *"What I don't know, I don't miss."*

Avoiding her brother-in-law had strained their relationship. She'd spent years believing what she read in the tabloids, and never bothered to ask Griffin if the stories about him were true. She'd fallen victim to a very human fault—believing what you read.

A deep voice, on an even lower register than Griffin's, reached her as she walked into the living room. Keith Ennis appeared taller, larger than the images she'd seen on television. She'd suggested Sabrina and Layla remain in their rooms until the ballplayer's arrival.

Griffin approached Belinda, beckoning. "Come, darling. I want to introduce you to a client who's also a good friend. Keith, this is Belinda Eaton. Belinda, Keith Ennis."

Belinda was too starstruck to register Griffin's endearment as she smiled at the larger-than-life superstar ballplayer. His sparkling raven-black eyes, shaved head, mahogany-hued smooth skin and trimmed silky mustache and goatee were mesmerizing.

She offered him her hand. "It's a pleasure to meet you."

Keith raised the delicate hand that he had swallowed up in his much larger one. "I can't believe Rice has been holding out on me," he crooned, winking, his baritone voice lowering seductively. "Where has he been hiding you?" he asked Belinda.

A rush of heat stung her cheeks. "I've been around."

Griffin looped a proprietary arm around Belinda's waist. "Sorry, man, but she's not available."

"If the lovely lady is unavailable, then why isn't there a ring on her finger, Rice?"

Belinda grimaced when she felt the bite of Griffin's fingers as they tightened on her waist. She flashed Keith a tight smile. "Please excuse me. I'm going upstairs to get Sabrina and Layla so they can meet you before the others arrive."

Belinda mentioning his meeting Griffin's nieces reminded Keith why he'd come to his attorney's home. His team had played a Saturday afternoon game, and he'd planned to unwind at his condo with the woman who usually kept him occupied during home games. However, Griffin got him to change his mind and his plans when he gave him a generous check as a donation to his alma mater.

Keith's gaze lingered briefly on Belinda Eaton before coming back to rest on Griffin's scowling face. "Look, man, I know I was out of line."

"You were." The two words were cold, exacting.

Keith recoiled as if he'd been struck. "Will you accept my apology?"

The seconds ticked off, the silence swelling and growing more uncomfortable with each tick. Griffin's face was a glowering mask of controlled fury. His client had stepped over the line. He'd taken Keith Ennis, a naturally talented athlete from a disadvantaged Baltimore neighborhood to instant superstar status with a five-year multimillion-dollar contract, along with high-profile product endorsements.

Griffin was normally laid-back, quick to smile, slow

to anger and willing to give anyone three strikes. Unfortunately, Keith Ennis had just used up one of his three. He angled his head. "That's something I'm going to have to think about. Can I get you something to drink?" he asked in the same breath.

Keith flashed a tremulous grin. "Sure."

Layla and Sabrina stared at their sport idol, tonguetied as Griffin snapped pictures of them shaking hands with Keith, flanking him when they posed as a group picture and when he autographed their brag books. The ballplayer, seeking redemption for his misstep, signed autographs for their teachers and fellow students. Clutching their treasured memorabilia to their chests, the sisters raced upstairs to text their friends.

Griffin and Belinda became the consummate host and hostess as they greeted guests with exotic cocktails and hors d'oeuvres. The Moroccan-style meatballs, deviled eggs with capers, mini crab cakes and beluga caviar on toast points were the highlight of the cocktail hour.

It didn't take Belinda long to understand why her sister liked socializing at Griffin's house. Excellent food, top-shelf liquor, friendly, outgoing guests and an attentive host made for certain success.

The thirtysomething crowd included college classmates, frat brothers and three newlywed couples. She knew a few of the guests were surprised to see her as hostess, but they soon got used to it. The music, which included old-school and new-school jams, had several couples up and dancing when everyone filed out of the dining room to the back porch.

It was ten o'clock when Keith bid his farewell, saying

he had to get up early for batting practice. Others followed suit over the next hour. Griffin paid and tipped the bartender, the chef and waitstaff, then led Belinda out to the patio, seating her on a cushioned chaise. The outdoor fireplace emitted enough heat to warm the mid-forty-degree temperature. Dozens of candles lining a long wooden table flickered, competing with millions of stars in the clear night sky.

Belinda slipped off her heels. "I'm going to need a throw or a blanket," she said, as Griffin joined her on the chaise.

Griffin nuzzled her neck. "I'll warm you up." Without warning, he effortlessly lifted her so that she sat between his outstretched legs. "Lean back against me."

Fatigue swept over her, and she closed her eyes. "It was a nice little get-together."

"It was nice," Griffin said in agreement, as he, too, closed his eyes.

She opened her eyes and peered up at him over her shoulder. "Some of your friends were somewhat surprised when you introduced me as your hostess. Were they perhaps expecting to see you with some other woman?"

Griffin opened his eyes. "I don't know what they expected, Belinda, because I've never concerned myself with how other folks see me. If I did, then I'd stop being who I am. And I deliberately didn't introduce you as my brother's sister-in-law because I felt it was none of their business."

"Did you tell Keith that I'm the girls' aunt?"

"Nope."

"Do you plan on telling him?"

"Nope."

"Why are you so monosyllabic?"

Using a minimum of effort and movement, Griffin changed positions until Belinda lay under him. "I don't feel very much like talking, Miss Eaton, because I'd rather do this."

She knew Griffin was going to kiss her, but was helpless to stop him. The truth was she didn't want to stop him. She'd lost count of the number of times she'd replayed him kissing her over and over—in and out of bed. Griffin had ignited a spark that grew hotter and more intense each time she saw him. A part of her wanted him to stay away—the sensible Belinda. Then there was the other Belinda—the sexually frustrated woman who hadn't slept with a man in three years.

Blood-pounding desire rushed through her veins. Her lips parted, she swallowed Griffin's warm, moist breath as his mouth covered hers in a hungry joining that left them tearing at each other's clothes. Belinda grasped the back of his sweater, pulling it up from his waist and baring flesh in her journey to get to know every part of Griffin Rice. She'd become addicted to him, his scent and the hard contours of his toned, slender body.

Griffin kissed Belinda with an outward calm that belied his hunger to take her—on the chaise and without protection. One hand slipped under her blouse, while the other slid up her inner thighs. The heat coming from between her legs was an inferno. Belinda was on fire, the flames spreading and racing out of control. He fastened his mouth over a breast, the nipple hardening when he suckled her through the cup of her lace bra.

"You are exquisite," he whispered, pressing his groin to hers so she could feel how much he wanted and needed her.

Looping her arms under Griffin's shoulders, Belinda

held on to him as if he were her lifeline while waves of ecstasy rocked her like a ship in a storm. He suckled one breast, then the other before trailing moist kisses down her belly. She was hot, then cold as Griffin released the zipper on her slacks, pushing them down her thighs; his head replaced his hands as he pressed his face to the apex of her legs.

Griffin inhaled the womanly essence through the scrap of silk. His longing to be inside Belinda bordered on insanity, but sanity won out when he moved up the length of her quivering body, his heart pounding in his chest like a jackhammer. He sat up, swinging his legs over the side of the chaise.

"One of these days we're going to finish this," he promised.

Belinda nodded rather than speak. She was afraid, afraid that she would beg Griffin to make love to her on the chaise and out in the open where Sabrina or Layla could possibly discover them. Raising her hips, she eased up and zipped her slacks and adjusted her top. An owl hooted in the distance as she reached for her shoes.

She stood up and stared at the outline of broad shoulders in the muted darkness. Griffin was so still he could've been a statue. "Good night, Griffin, and don't forget to put out the candles."

Getting up from the chaise, Griffin smiled at the woman who'd wound herself into his life and his heart. "Good night, Lindy."

Chapter 7

"Miss Ferguson, please take your seat. Mr. Evans, you know the rules. No hats or do-rags." The high school administration had banned cell phones and do-rags for male students while classes were in session. Students had to wear picture IDs, and they'd installed metal detectors because of an incident in which one student stabbed and killed another with a knife he'd concealed under his cap. Their attempt to ban gang colors was voted down by the school board, and the result was a proliferation of red, blue and gold bandannas and jackets.

Belinda knew her students were restless and looking forward to spring break, and she was no exception. She would use the week to sleep in late, weed her flower garden, clean out her closets and hopefully catch up on her reading.

Sabrina and Layla, who attended a private school, had begun their spring break two days before their public school counterpart. They were on a week-long class trip that would take them from Washington, D.C., to Williamsburg, Virginia, and finally the Gettysburg National Military Park before returning. With the girls away and Griffin in Chicago on business, if it hadn't been for Cecil and Nigel's barking the house would've been as silent as a tomb. The past two mornings she'd gotten up early to take care of the puppies, and she knew she couldn't linger after classes because she needed to get home to see after them.

"Miss Eaton, tell Brent to get out of my seat."

Belinda let out an audible sigh. "Mr. Wiley, please find your own seat."

Brent Wiley took his time sliding off the chair to sit on another in the next row, all the while glaring at the petite, dark-haired female student with whom he had a love-hate, on-again, off-again relationship since the school year began. Their enmity escalated when it was rumored that Petra Rutherford was dating a rival gang member.

He pointed a finger at her. "I'm gonna fix you, ho!"

Petra Rutherford jumped up. "Your momma's a ho, bitch!"

Belinda had had enough. "Mr. Wiley, out!"

Brent Wiley knew the drill. Whenever Miss Eaton ordered a student out of her classroom it meant a visit to the dean. It also meant a call home, and that meant big trouble for him. His old man was on his back because some of his friends were in a gang, but what Brent couldn't understand was that his pops had been in a gang when he was in his teens, did a bid in prison but after he was paroled found religion. Pushing back his chair, Brent stood up. He nodded to another boy, pulled up his baggy jeans, then gathered his books and left the classroom.

Belinda waited until she had everyone's attention. She glared at Petra. "Miss Rutherford, count yourself lucky, because you also should be in the dean's office."

Petra rolled her eyes. "I ain't gonna let nobody call me a ho," she mumbled under her breath.

Leaning against the front of her desk, Belinda crossed her legs at the ankles. The girls sitting in the front row glanced down at her shoes and smiled at one another. She knew the female students in particular monitored what she wore. On several occasions they'd ask if a jacket or blouse was new because they hadn't seen it before, which led Belinda to believe they were cataloguing her wardrobe.

She felt it important to wear business attire, unlike those teachers who sometimes wore jeans and sweats. Today she wore taupe linen gabardine slacks with a white silk man-tailored shirt and waist-length tan suede jacket. Her footwear was a pair of brown leather pumps. Not only was she an educator but also a role model for her students. In order to be a professional she also had to look the part.

"Yesterday I gave out copies of three things—two newspaper cartoons and one photograph. I wanted you to analyze them and write a paragraph on what message the cartoonist and photographer are trying to express." A hand went up in the back of the room. "Yes, Mr. Sanchez."

"The photograph with the man holding a sign with Burn All Reds is expressing his hatred for communists."

"You're right, Mr. Sanchez. But couldn't he just as easily been protesting fascists, immigrants or even the police officers you see in the photograph?"

"No way, Miss Eaton. I showed my grandpa the picture and he said the woman holding the sign, Rosenberg Traitors Must Die For Their Crime, was because the Rosenbergs who were communists sold the atom bomb secrets to the Russians."

Belinda smiled. It wasn't easy to engage her students about what they considered "old news" that had nothing to do with their lives. "Did your grandfather tell you what happened to the Rosenbergs?"

Jaime Sanchez flashed a wide smile. "They lit up the commie bastards in the electric chair."

Belinda shifted so the students wouldn't see her smirk as they laughed loudly. She didn't think she would ever get used to their colorful language. She tried to keep the use of expletives in her classroom to a minimum, but knew she was fighting a losing cause.

"Yes," she said, "they were found guilty of spying for the Soviet Union and sentenced to death by execution. Does anyone else have a comment about the photograph?" No hands went up as students lounged in their seats as if in their living rooms. "I need someone to analyze the cartoon from the *Birmingham News* dated June 27, 2002. It's a picture of Uncle Sam with a copy of the Constitution, holding a pencil with the word *security* stamped on it. Uncle Sam's thinking, *So...where do I draw the line?*

"What is the central focus of this cartoon drawn after September 11, 2001? Is the cartoonist saying that the United States should abandon the Constitution, or..." Belinda's words stopped when she saw a student get up and open the window. "Sit down, Mr. Greer," she ordered when he reached out the window.

The words were barely off her tongue when sunlight

glinted on a shiny object in the student's hand. "Everybody get down!" Belinda screamed before an explosion and flash of light changed the lives of all in the classroom.

Televised footage of past school shootings came back with vivid clarity. Belinda struggled to remember the protocol for such an incident. How was it she could remember the tragic faces of parents and students but not what she'd been told if a similar situation occurred at her school?

It was the second gunshot that jolted her into action as shards of glass and plaster rained down on those huddled under desks. She had to alert the office to initiate an immediate school lockdown. The wail of approaching sirens drowned out the sounds of students' screams when two more shots shattered the windows. The classroom was under siege as shell casings littered the floor.

Belinda knew it was impossible to reach the wall phone installed in each classroom without exposing herself to the gunman. Crawling on her belly, she opened the lower drawer of the desk, grabbing her handbag. She found her cell and punched in three digits. Her voice was surprisingly calm when she told the 911 operator what was happening. The operator told her that someone else had called in the gunfire and first responders would be there in minutes.

She placed another call—to her mother—and then prayed.

Griffin sat at the conference room table with the senior vice president of an upscale clothing manufacturer, staring numbly at downtown Chicago through the wall-to-wall window in a towering office building.

Oakley Donovan wanted to offer GR Sports Enter-

prises, Limited, a lucrative seven-figure deal for a flam-
boyant tennis pro to model sportswear for next year's
spring and summer line. He would've agreed to the
deal, yet held out because he wanted Oakley Donovan
to commit to all four seasons. A deal which should've
been inked in one day but was now into its fourth.

Before he boarded the flight to Chicago, Griffin and
Belinda saw their nieces off as they got the bus with
twenty-eight other seventh graders for their class trip. She
drove him to the airport, and his flight touched down at
O'Hare forty minutes before his scheduled meeting.
Instead of checking into a hotel he took a taxi directly to
Donovan's office building where he was told that Oakley
Donovan's wife had gone into labor, giving birth to a baby
boy, and he regretfully had to postpone their meeting.

Griffin informed Donovan's executive assistant that
he could be reached at the Palmer House in the event that
the new father wanted to set up another meeting. During
the two days it took for Donovan to reschedule, Griffin
attended a Cubs versus Mets baseball game at Wrigley
Field, sent Donovan's wife a gift basket for the newborn
and sampled the much-touted Chicago hot dog and deep-
dish pizza. He became a tourist, picking up souvenir
caps and T-shirts for Sabrina, Layla and Belinda.

He'd planned to spend the week at Belinda's house
if he hadn't had the Chicago meeting. Having her so
close whenever she slept under his roof and kissing her
under the guise of a greeting had begun to test the limits
of his patience, of which he had very little.

Griffin laced his fingers together and counted slowly
to ten. "It's unfortunate you'll only commit to the spring
and summer, because if you decide to use Keats for subsequent seasons, then the price goes up exponentially."

Oakley Donovan found it hard to concentrate. He still hadn't recovered from witnessing the birth of his first son, whom his third and much younger wife insisted on naming after him. "How much more, Rice?"

Griffin's head came up and he stared at the man, who at fifty-nine, should've been rocking his grandchildren instead of a newborn. Oakley Donovan reminded him of a shark—he was all teeth. But he wasn't taken in by the wide grin and genteel manner. Under the custom-made shirt, handmade silk tie and tailored suit beat the cold heart of a shark. Donovan sold a likeness of a model to a cigarette manufacturer without securing a release from the model. It took a decade for the model to settle for an amount, which had made him quite wealthy. He knew Oakley wanted tennis ace David Keats to model his clothing line and Griffin was prepared to hold out until Oakley met his price.

"Double, but only if I'm feeling generous."

Donovan's Adam's apple bobbed up and down like a buoy in choppy water. "And if you're not feeling generous, Rice?"

"It quadruples."

Streaks of red crept up Donovan's neck to his smooth-shaven cheeks. "You're joking, aren't you?"

Griffin shook his head slowly. "No. I'm not very good when it comes to telling jokes." He almost felt sorry for the man who was the epitome of sophistication. It was easy to see why Oakley Donovan was able to attract women half his age.

The door to the conference opened and a woman with salt-and-pepper hair nodded to her boss. "I'm sorry to disturb you, Mr. Donovan, but I thought you'd want to know that there's been a shooting at a high school in

An Important Message from the Publisher

Dear Reader,

Because you've chosen to read one of our fine novels, I'd like to say "thank you"! And, as a special way to say thank you, I'm offering to send you two more Kimani™ Romance novels and two surprise gifts – absolutely FREE! These books will keep it real with true-to-life African American characters that turn up the heat and sizzle with passion.

Please enjoy the free books and gifts with our compliments...

Linda Gill

Publisher, Kimani Press

Peel off Seal and Place Inside...

We'd like to send you two free books to introduce you to Kimani™ Romance. These novels feature strong, sexy women, and African-American heroes that are charming, loving and true. Our authors fill each page with exceptional dialogue, exciting plot twists, and enough sizzling romance to keep you riveted until the very end!

KIMANI ROMANCE ... LOVE'S ULTIMATE DESTINATION

Your two books have a combined cover price of $11.98, but are yours **FREE!** We'll even send you two wonderful surprise gifts. You can't lose!

2 Free Bonus Gifts!

We'll send you two wonderful surprise gifts, (worth about $10) absolutely FREE, just for giving KIMANI ROMANCE books a try! Don't miss out — **MAIL THE REPLY CARD TODAY!**

www.KimaniPress.com

THE EDITOR'S "THANK YOU" FREE GIFTS INCLUDE:

▶ Two Kimani™ Romance Novels
▶ Two exciting surprise gifts

YES! I have placed my Editor's "thank you" Free Gifts seal in the space provided at right. Please send me 2 FREE books, and my 2 FREE Mystery Gifts. I understand that I am under no obligation to purchase anything further, as explained on the back of this card.

EDITOR'S
FREE GIFTS
SEAL
"THANK YOU"

168 XDL EVGW   368 XDL EVJ9

FIRST NAME

LAST NAME

ADDRESS

APT.#

CITY

STATE/PROV.

ZIP/POSTAL CODE

Thank You!

Offer limited to one per household and not valid to current subscribers of Kimani Romance books. **Your Privacy** - Kimani Press is committed to protecting your privacy. Our Privacy Policy is available online at www.KimaniPress.com or upon request from the Reader Service. From time to time we make our lists of customers available to reputable third parties who may have a product or service of interest to you. If you would prefer for us not to share your name and address, please check here ☐. ® and ™ are trademarks owned and used by the trademark owner and/or its licensee. © 2008 Kimani Press.

◀ DETACH AND MAIL CARD TODAY! ▼

(K-ROM-09)

Accepting your 2 free books and 2 free gifts places you under no obligation to buy anything. You may keep the books and gifts and return the shipping statement marked "cancel." If you do not cancel, about a month later we'll send you 4 additional books and bill you just $4.69 each in the U.S., or $5.24 each in Canada, plus 25¢ shipping and handling per book and applicable taxes if any." You may cancel at any time, but if you choose to continue, every month we'll send you 4 more books, which you may either purchase at the discount price or return to us and cancel your subscription.

*Terms and prices subject to change without notice. Sales tax applicable in N.Y. Canadian residents will be charged applicable provincial taxes and GST. Offer not valid in Quebec. All orders subject to approval. Credit or debit balances in a customer's account(s) may be offset by any other outstanding balance owed by or to the customer. Offer available while quantities last. Books received may vary. Please allow 4 to 6 weeks for delivery.

If offer card is missing write to: The Reader Service, 3010 Walden Ave., P.O. Box 1867, Buffalo, NY 14240-1867

BUSINESS REPLY MAIL
FIRST-CLASS MAIL   PERMIT NO. 717   BUFFALO, NY

POSTAGE WILL BE PAID BY ADDRESSEE

THE READER SERVICE
3010 WALDEN AVE
PO BOX 1867
BUFFALO NY 14240-9952

NO POSTAGE
NECESSARY
IF MAILED
IN THE
UNITED STATES

Philadelphia. So far, the newscasters haven't identified the school."

Oakley's teenage daughters from his second marriage lived and went to school in Philadelphia. The color drained from his face at the same time Griffin stood up and pushed back his chair.

Griffin met Oakley's wild-eyed stare. "Do you have a television?" His first thought was of Belinda, who taught at one of the most notorious high schools in the city.

"Yes. In my office."

Minutes later, the two men stood in front of a wall-mounted screen, their gazes fixed on the images of uniformed police in riot gear taking up positions around the perimeter of the school. Fear, stark and vivid, seized Griffin as he read the crawl at the bottom of the screen. A police negotiator had made contact with a lone gunman who was holding his teacher and classmates hostage.

Reaching for his BlackBerry, Griffin punched in a number on speed dial. "Answer the phone, Belinda," he whispered, but the call went to voice mail. His next call was to Roberta Eaton. "Roberta, Griffin. Have you heard anything?"

"Belinda called to let me know that she's okay. She must have turned off her cell phone because it's going straight to voice mail. I've been on my knees praying ever since she called. I don't know what I'd do if I lost another child."

"You're not going to lose her, Roberta."

"I pray you're right. Where are you, Griffin?"

"Chicago."

"When are you coming back?"

"I'll be back as soon as I can book a return flight."

Oakley pulled his gaze away from the television. "Thank goodness it's not my daughters' school."

Griffin glared at the man who was responsible for taking a small apparel company from virtual obscurity to compete with Ralph Lauren and Tommy Hilfiger. "Lucky for you," he drawled facetiously. "The woman I love teaches at that school."

Oakley looked contrite. "Maybe I can help you out. I'll have my driver take you back to your hotel where you can pick up your luggage. From there he'll take you to the airport. The company jet will fly you directly into Philly." He turned to his assistant. "Call the pilot and have him fuel and ready the jet. He'll have one passenger going to Philadelphia International. Also call Leonard and have him bring the car around." He smiled at Griffin. "You better get going, Rice. Call me when things settle down."

Griffin shook the businessman's hand before sprinting out the door. It wasn't until he was seated on the leather seat in the small private jet that he realized he'd spoken his thoughts aloud.

He'd fallen in love with Belinda Eaton.

The jet landed on a private runway at Philadelphia International and Griffin rang Belinda's cell phone. Again it went to voice mail. He stopped in a terminal long enough to watch a reporter on CNN recap the events of the school shooting and standoff that lasted less than two hours. A police spokesperson reported they had taken one suspect into custody and details of the incident would be made public at a city hall press conference later that evening. Classes were canceled for the next two days and counselors would be available for students, faculty and staff.

He called Roberta again, who told him that Belinda stopped by to prove she was okay.

"Where is she now?"

"Home. I tried to get her to stay, but she said she needed to be alone."

"That's what she doesn't need," he argued.

"I agree, Griffin. Perhaps she'll listen to you."

He smiled for the first time in hours. "I'll take care of her."

There was a noticeable pause. "I know you will."

Griffin flagged down a taxi and gave him Belinda's address. He wasn't convinced that she was all right until he saw her for himself. The driver pulled away from the curbside as if he were taking a road test.

Griffin tapped the Plexiglas partition. "Hey, my man, can't you drive any faster?"

The cabbie glanced over his shoulder. "I take it you're in a hurry?"

Griffin flashed a supercilious grin. "Yes, I am." The taxi driver maneuvered around a slow-moving van, accelerated and took the road leading out of the airport. Pressing his back against the worn seat, Griffin closed his eyes. "Thanks."

Why, he asked himself, did it have to take a life-and-death situation for him to open his eyes? His relationship with Belinda had been rocky at first until they realized fighting each other was not healthy for their nieces.

He would never replace Grant as their father no matter how hard he tried. But, on the other hand, Belinda had slipped into her role as mother as if she were born to it. Perhaps it had something to do with her being a teacher. She understood children needed and wanted boundaries if they were to feel secure. Sabrina and Layla were given a list of chores they had to fulfill and it was on a rare occasion that a task went undone.

Griffin mentally rehearsed all the things he wanted to say to Belinda but when the taxi maneuvered into the driveway leading to her house they were forgotten when he saw her Volvo parked behind his Lexus.

He felt like a mechanical windup toy when he paid the driver and gathered his bags and mounted the porch steps. Lengthening afternoon shadows shaded a portion of the porch where Belinda liked to sit out in the evening to watch the sun set. She claimed it was her favorite time of the day—the period between dusk and sunset when the world seemed to settle down for the night. It was only when he'd joined her one night that he felt what she felt—a calming peace where poverty, hunger and disease, for a brief nanosecond, did not exist.

Reaching for a key, he inserted it into the lock and pushed open the door. A lamp on the table in the entryway emitted a soft glow as he left his bags in the corner next to a coatrack. Placing one foot in front of the other, Griffin walked through the living room and down the narrow hallway that led to Belinda's bedroom. The clothes she'd worn that day were on a chair in the dressing room.

Retracing his steps, he headed for the staircase, then stopped when he heard barking coming from the direction of the kitchen. When they were home alone, Nigel and Cecil were given the run of their cage with food and water in an area between the kitchen and pantry.

Griffin checked on the puppies, who, when they saw him, started whining to get out. The bottle attached to the cage was filled with water, the food dishes filled and the bottom of the cage was lined with clean pads. He smiled and shook his head. Despite all that she'd encountered, Belinda had still found time to take care of the puppies. She took care of everyone, but there was no one to take care of her.

Griffin had promised his brother that he would take care of his children and he'd also promised Roberta that he would take care of Belinda—and he would. He took the back staircase to the second floor. The door to the bathroom stood open and when he peered in Griffin was stunned by the scene unfolding before him.

Belinda lay in the bathtub filled with bubbles, sipping from a wineglass. A half-empty bottle of wine rested on a low table next to the tub. Music flowed from a radio on a corner shelf. Leaning against the doorframe, he stared at the moisture dotting her face. Wisps from her upswept hairdo clung to her forehead and cheek, but she didn't seem to mind getting her hair wet.

"Would you like company?"

Belinda sat up, nearly upsetting the table with the wine when her elbow knocked into it. "What are you doing here?" she asked in a breathless whisper.

Straightening, Griffin gave her a tender smile. "I came to see if you're all right."

Placing the glass on the table, Belinda slipped lower into the water. "Of course I'm all right. Why wouldn't I be?"

A slight frown creased his forehead. Had she forgotten what had happened at her school that afternoon, or had she deliberately blocked it out of her mind? "Are you sure you're okay, Belinda?"

"Of course I am! I wish everyone would stop asking me if I'm all right. I'm alive, Griffin. Isn't that enough?"

The tears Belinda had managed to keep at bay

pricked the backs of her eyelids, but she was helpless to stop them once they fell. Fat, hot tears rolled down her face and into the froth of bubbles.

Taking off his jacket and tie, Griffin dropped them on a chair and went to his knees. He reached down and lifted Belinda into his arms. "Cry and let it all out. I'm here," he repeated over and over until her sobs lessened to soft hiccuping sounds. It was then that he wrapped her naked body in a bath sheet and carried her downstairs to her bedroom.

Placing her on the bed, his body following hers down, they lay together, his chest against her back. "Feeling better, baby?"

"I think I'm drunk, Griffin. I drank more than half the bottle of wine."

He kissed the nape of her neck. "Go to sleep."

"All the kids were screaming."

"Don't, baby. Go to sleep. We'll talk about it tomorrow."

"Will you stay with me tonight?"

"Of course. I'll stay with you tonight, tomorrow night and every night after that."

"Do you know what?" Belinda's words were slurring.

"What, darling?" A silence ensued, and Griffin thought she'd fallen asleep.

"I like you, Griffin Rice."

There came another prolonged silence before he spoke again. "And I love you, Belinda Eaton." The sound of snoring answered his confession. She'd fallen asleep.

He dimmed the table lamp to the lowest setting, removed the bath sheet and pulled the sheet up over her body. He wanted to stay in bed with Belinda, but it was too much of a temptation. If and when he did make love to her he wanted her willing and not under the influence.

Griffin lost track of time as he sat on the side of the bed, watching her sleep. When he did finally get up it was to let the water out of the bathtub, cork the wine bottle, and turn off the radio and light.

He sat in the living room staring numbly at the television as the mayor, police department and school officials all took credit for quickly defusing a volatile situation without loss of life.

Reporters had interviewed students who speculated as to what had had happened but they were unable to get the true story because the students in the American history and government classroom where the shooting and standoff had occurred refused to speak to the press.

Griffin felt a sinking feeling in the pit of his stomach. He knew the student with the gun was Belinda's.

Chapter 8

Bright sunlight coming in through the windows and the fragrant smell of coffee greeted Belinda when she sat up in bed. She peered down at her naked breasts and realization dawned. Griffin had come, and he'd put her in bed. Reaching for the silk wrap at her feet, she pushed her arms into the sleeves and belted it. The sour taste on her tongue was a reminder of the wine she'd drunk the night before. Right now she needed to brush her teeth and rinse her mouth, shower and get dressed. She walked out of the bedroom and made her way to the half bath off the kitchen.

Belinda's stomach did a flip-flop when she ran into Griffin. "Good morning," she mumbled, not breaking stride.

Griffin smiled. "Good morning, beautiful." He'd gotten up early to take care of the puppies, and instead of going back to the sleeper-sofa he decided to surprise Belinda with breakfast in bed.

"I'll be out in a few minutes," she said, closing the bathroom door behind her.

He waited for Belinda to emerge from the small bathroom, handing her a mug of steaming coffee. She smelled like mint. "Take this and go back to bed. Breakfast should be ready in about ten minutes."

Belinda pressed her lips to his stubbly jaw. "I have a confession to make."

Griffin resisted the urge to kiss the full, lush lips inches from his own. If he knew it would've been a mistake to sleep with her the night before, he was more than aware this morning that if he kissed Belinda Eaton he wouldn't finish breakfast, and he would carry her into the bedroom, put her on her back and be inside her before he'd be able to stop himself.

He closed his eyes, shutting out the image of her mussed hair falling provocatively around her scrubbed face. Griffin knew what lay under the silky fabric, and if she didn't leave—now—he doubted whether he'd be able to control the lower portion of his body.

"What is it?" His question sounded angry.

Tears filled Belinda's eyes. "I lied to my mother yesterday when I told her I was all right. I wasn't, Griffin. When that kid fired that gun all I thought about were mothers having to bury their children. And if he'd killed me, then it would be the second time in less than six months for my mother."

Griffin eased the mug from her fingers and put it on the cooking island. He cradled her face in his hands. "If you want to talk about it, I'll listen. But we don't have to do it now. You're going to eat, and then pack a bag. I'm bringing you home with me."

Belinda shook her head. "I don't—"

"I don't want you to fight with me, Lindy," he interrupted. "Now, take your coffee and get into bed."

She took the mug. "Why are you trying to sound like a daddy?"

"That's because I am a daddy."

Belinda hadn't walked out of the kitchen when the doorbell rang. The sound set off a chorus of barking from the Yorkies. She glanced over at the clock on the microwave. It wasn't eight o'clock.

Griffin held up a hand. "I'll see who it is."

He didn't want her answering the door wearing next to nothing. After showering, he'd slipped into a pair of jeans and T-shirt. After his first sleep-over he left several changes of clothes, underwear and grooming products at Belinda's house.

He opened the door to find two conservatively dressed young black men standing on the porch. "Whatever you're selling we're not buying."

The taller of the two held up a hand. "Wait, mister. We're reporters and we'd like to talk to Belinda Eaton about the shooting incident in her classroom yesterday."

"Miss Eaton is not home," Griffin lied smoothly. "Now, I'd appreciate it if you'd leave."

"But isn't that her car?" the other man asked, pointing to the Volvo with her high school faculty parking sticker affixed to the rear bumper.

A muscle in Griffin's jaw tensed as he clenched his teeth. "Get off this property before I have you arrested for trespassing."

"Look, my brother, we're just trying to get a story for our college newspaper."

Griffin bit back a smile. "Oh, now I'm your brother. What college?"

"Temple," they said in unison.

"Do you have a press badge?"

"Sorry."

"I forgot mine."

"What kind of idiot do you take me for, *my brothers?*" Griffin shouted. "Any self-respecting, aspiring journalist would have a press badge. I graduated Temple even before you two were zygotes, and I remember that anyone who worked on the college paper carried identification. I'm Miss Eaton's attorney and as such I've instructed her not to speak to the press. I'm going to give you some advice for which I usually charge my clients seven hundred-fifty an hour." He glared at the two young men. "Never play the race card, because it's immature and cheesy. Good day, gentlemen."

Stepping back, Griffin closed the door, leaving them staring at the door, then each other. Someone wanted an eyewitness account of what had occurred in her classroom and they were willing to pay to get it. If Belinda wanted to talk to the media she would've done it yesterday, unless she was instructed not to say anything by school officials.

The school board had closed the high school, giving students two extra days of spring break. Griffin would use the time to help Belinda heal, and hopefully forget that she could've possibly become another school shooting statistic.

* * *

"Why are you treating me as if I were an invalid?"

Griffin tightened his hold under Belinda's legs as he carried her to the patio. "Haven't you ever had a man spoil you?"

"No—I mean, yes."

"Which is it, Lindy?"

Belinda closed her eyes, shutting out his intense stare. She hadn't been given a choice when Griffin told her to pack a bag with enough clothes to last a week, adding that she should include a few for dining out. He put Nigel and Cecil into the crate he stored in the back of his SUV and called Roberta to let her know that he was taking her daughter to his house to get away from the hysteria. They made one stop—to the post office to fill out the form to stop the delivery of her mail. Smiling and looking quite smug, Griffin headed out in a westerly direction towards Paoli.

She opened her eyes when he lowered her to the chaise. "I don't want to be spoiled."

Leaning over her prone figure, Griffin kissed the end of her nose. "What do you want?"

"I wanted to be respected as a grown woman, Griffin, and not someone who can't think for herself."

He folded his body down beside her. "You think I don't respect you? If I didn't respect you, Belinda, I would've taken advantage of you last night. You'd had too much to drink, and even though you claim you can beat me up with one arm tied behind your back I doubt whether your martial arts training would've become a factor." He leaned closer. "Black belt notwithstanding, physically you're no match for me."

For a long moment, Belinda looked back at Griffin,

mesmerized by the stubble on his jaw and chin and asking herself which Griffin Rice she liked better—the urbane attorney who wore tailored suits and Italian footwear, or the laid-back unshaven man who was visually delicious in a pair of jeans and T-shirt. Seeing him dressed down with the sunlight providing a back-light for his rich olive-hued face answered her question. She much preferred this version.

"I know. I just said that to scare you."

His eyebrows shot up. "You don't have a black belt?"

"Oh, I have the belt."

"Why, then, did you want to scare me?"

Belinda hesitated, choosing her words carefully. "I didn't want you to get too close to me."

"Why, Lindy?"

Her delicate jaw tightened. "Because the only man I ever let get that close hurt me physically and emotion-ally, and I swore it would never happen again."

Griffin placed a hand on the side of her face. "What did he do to you?"

Belinda formed her thoughts in some semblance of order. What she was going to tell Griffin was something she'd never revealed to anyone, including her parents. The incident was branded in her memory for eternity, changing and making her into what she'd become.

"Joel Thurman and I started dating in high school, and when it came time to go to college he switched his first choice so we could be together."

"Were you sleeping with him?"

Belinda nodded. "My first time was the night of our senior prom. We both lived on campus, and he slept in my dorm room more than he did his own. But everything changed when I joined a study group and he thought I was cheating on him with another boy. We argued constantly because he wanted me to quit the group."

"Did you?"

"No. The kids in the group were my friends, and if I'd left then it would prove I'd been cheating on him. One night he came to my room and found one of my study buddies sleeping in my bed. The boy had asked to lie down because he wasn't feeling well. Joel told me he was going to the library to pick up a book. I should've known something wasn't right when he said I'd better be alone when he got back.

"I woke Khaled and told him he had to leave. He'd come down with the flu and I had to get several guys to help get him back to his room. Joel returned, closed the door and told me that if he ever found me alone in my room with a man again he would kill me. He threw me on the bed, ripped off my panties and proceeded to rape me. I started to fight back until something told me not to move. When I went completely still, he pulled out, and all my martial arts training came back as if I were in a competition.

"What amazed me is that no one came to see what the noise was all about. I literally kicked his ass all around the room. It was the first and last time I ever felt like murdering another human being. Joel jumped out a second-story window to escape. After I came to my senses, I straightened up my room, then called Myles, asking him to come and get me. Three days later I went back to school, cleaned out my room and moved off campus."

"What happened to Joel?"

"He broke his right arm in the fall, but told everyone he'd slipped and fell headfirst down a flight of stairs."

"Did he move off campus, too?"

Belinda shook her head. "He stayed while I commuted. Every time he saw me he went in the opposite direction."

Now Griffin had the answer to why Belinda moved back home. "You didn't think about charging him with attempted rape?"

"No. If I'd told my brother that Joel tried to rape me he would've killed him. He took his role as older brother to three sisters very seriously. It's a wonder that Grant was able to get close to Donna after my brother's brutal interrogation."

"That's because Rice men don't scare easily."

Belinda lowered her gaze to stare at him from under her lashes. "Does anything frighten you?"

Cradling her face between his palms, Griffin leaned even closer. "Not having you in my life frightens the hell out of me."

Her lashes flew up, her heart beating like that of a tiny, frightened bird. "But I am in your life, Griffin. We'll be together for the next eleven years."

"A marriage of eleven years isn't that long," he teased.

"It doesn't matter because we're not married."

He nodded. "You're right."

They weren't married and Griffin wondered if he or Belinda would ever marry. In eleven years they would be forty-eight and forty-three, respectively. Not too old to marry, but in his opinion a bit old to become parents. But with the advances in modern medicine, many forty-year-olds were giving birth to healthy babies.

Realizing he'd fallen in love with Belinda Eaton was an awakening and sobering experience. It left him reeling from a sense of fulfillment that graduating

college, law school, passing the bar or negotiating multimillion-dollar contracts couldn't match.

Griffin closed his eyes for several seconds. "Would
you like to get married?" he asked, staring at the woman
who unwittingly had captured his heart. The brilliant
sunlight flattered her smooth skin, affording it the ap-
pearance of rich dark-chocolate mousse.

Belinda's eyebrows lifted. "Are you proposing or
asking a question?"

Griffin would've said proposing if he was certain
Belinda was in love with him. Admitting that she liked
him wasn't tantamount to a marriage proposal or a commitment to spend the rest of their lives together.

"I was asking a question," he said instead.

Belinda shrugged a shoulder. "I think I would one of
these days. But it can't be until the girls are legally
emancipated. It would be unfair to bring a new man into
their lives when they're so attached to you."

Now you're talking, he mused. That meant she wasn't
going to marry Sunshine—at least not for the next
eleven years. "I feel the same way about other women."

"I thought you didn't have other women."

"I *used* to see other women." He brushed a kiss over
her parted lips. "Do I detect a hint of jealousy?"

She wrinkled her nose. "Maybe a little."

"Now, why is that?" Griffin asked as he placed light
kisses at the corners of her mouth.

"Because I like you."

"I'm willing to wager that I like you more than you
like me."

Looping her arms under his shoulders, Belinda
leaned into the man who made her ache for him. While
she'd lain on the floor of the classroom, waiting for

death, she thought about her parents, brother, younger sister and her nieces who'd recently lost their parents and could possibly lose their aunt. Then, when she least expected it, images of Griffin Rice had swept over her. She'd recalled everything about him: his face, smile, the attractive cleft in his strong chin, his melodious baritone, the natural masculine scent of his bare skin that elicited erotic fantasies and his touch that ignited a fire only he could extinguish.

"It doesn't matter, Griffin, because I don't gamble."

He gave her a wink. "I do like you, Lindy Eaton."

She returned the wink. "Why don't you show me how much you like me."

Griffin was about to finish what they'd started and stopped so many times. He wanted Belinda so much that he couldn't remember when he didn't want her. She'd become as essential to him as breathing was to sustaining life. Reaching out, he swept her off the chaise and carried her into the house. Aside from Cecil and Nigel, who were huddled together in their cage asleep, there was just the two of them.

Belinda buried her face between the neck and shoulder of her soon-to-be lover, closing her eyes. She needed him to take away the hurt and pain that marred the good times in her life. As the third child, and the second daughter of Dwight and Roberta Eaton, she'd grown up loved and protected.

Then there was Joel Thurman, the young man to whom she'd given her most precious gift—her virginity—who'd shattered her trust in men. It took years before she felt secure enough to become involved with another man. Her second foray into the dating game started well but ended badly. She learned to never date someone with whom you work.

She was no longer a virgin and she didn't live or work with Griffin. He wasn't looking to get married and neither was she. They shared custody of their nieces, which meant they would always share a special bond that would continue beyond Sabrina and Layla's twenty-third birthdays. The bond was further strengthened because her sister had married his brother.

They were family.

Griffin concentrated on counting the number of steps that took him to his bedroom rather than think of the woman in his arms. His vow not to become involved with his nieces' godmother was shattered the first time he kissed her. He knew he'd been attracted to Belinda during their first encounter, which now seemed so long ago. Yet his ego hadn't allowed him to admit that a woman hadn't succumbed to his so-called charm. What had worked with so many women was wasted on Belinda Eaton. Most times she looked past him as if he didn't exist, or when she did meet his gaze he saw re-vulsion and indifference.

Annoyed because he liked her and she appeared to merely tolerate his presence, he thought she was stuck-up, a snob. What he hadn't known was that if she hadn't fought off her attacker, then she would've been a rape victim. If he'd known Joel Thurman at that time he would've sustained more serious injuries than a broken arm. Griffin would've broken his neck.

Belinda opened her eyes when she felt the firmness of the mattress under her body. She lay on a king-size bed with massive carved posts. Her gaze widened when Griffin moved over her, supporting his weight on his elbows.

Griffin studied her intently. "Let me know if you're ready to do this."

Belinda framed his lean face with her hands as a mysterious smile softened her mouth. "I was ready a long time ago, but I didn't know it."

She'd fallen in love with Griffin Rice on sight. She'd watched her sister with Grant, praying she could have the same with Griffin.

It was not to be. While she pined for him from afar he flitted from woman to woman like a modern-day Casanova. His rakish behavior had become a sobering awakening to her yearning for what she would never have, and in the end she concluded she hadn't been in love, but just infatuated with her brother-in-law.

Now, she wasn't so sure.

Chapter 9

Belinda felt a rush of desire, anticipation and a physical craving for the man who made her question why she'd been celibate and why she continued to deny the very reason she'd been born female.

Griffin's hands slipped under her T-shirt, gathering fabric as he began the task of baring her body. Her breath quickened, her chest rising and falling as his fingers traced the outline of her breasts through the sheer white bra. With a minimum of effort, he released the clasp, freeing the firm mounds of flesh.

His heated gaze caressed bared flesh. "You're more perfect than I'd imagined." He'd only caught a glimpse of her naked body the night before.

Griffin had waited years for Belinda, waited while the world changed, he'd changed and she'd changed from a reticent nineteen-year-old college student into a sensual, confident woman who kept him off balance. She'd had a sexual encounter that'd left scars, and he knew he had to get her to trust him if they were going to have a fulfilling love life.

His hands traced the curve of her midriff, the indentation of her waist and the flare of her hips. Lowering his head, he brushed his mouth over hers, moist breaths mingling, tongues tasting and fusing as banked passions stirred to life. Griffin wanted to take Belinda hard and fast but forced himself to go slow.

"I won't hurt you, baby. I'll never hurt you."

Belinda didn't know whether Griffin was talking about physical or emotional hurt. She knew instinctually that if he did hurt her it would be unintentional. His hands and mouth were doing things to her she'd forgotten, and she resisted the urge to move her hips. But her body refused to follow the dictates of her brain when she arched off the mattress with the intent of getting closer to him.

Her need, the urgency to feel him inside her, communicated itself to Griffin. Sitting back on his heels, he released the waistband and zipper on her jeans and eased them down her legs, the denim fabric joining her shirt and bra on the carpet beside the bed. All that remained was her bikini panties. They, too, joined the pile of clothing, and Griffin was able to see what layers of fabric had concealed from his inquisitive gaze.

He smiled. Belinda Eaton's body matched the exquisiteness of her face. Shapely calves, slender ankles and feet, flat belly, a narrow waist and rib cage he could span with both hands and a pair of firm breasts that didn't require the support of a bra to hold them up. His hungry, heated gaze lingered briefly on her parted lips before journeying down the length of her body and then reversing itself.

Belinda closed her eyes as a slow, warming desire raced through her body. She couldn't understand why Griffin continued to stare at her rather than make love to her. He knew she was waiting for him, that she'd been ready for him for what now seemed a lifetime ago. On the Friday or Saturday nights she'd sat home alone because she didn't have a date or had turned one down, she pondered where would she have been if she hadn't rebuffed Griffin Rice's subtle overtures. Would she still be single and childless if she hadn't declined his invitations?

She'd loved him from afar, but that love was bittersweet because she had gotten him by default. Fate had intervened and offered her a chance to be with the man she loved, if only temporarily. They were given eleven years to be together before going their separate ways to lead separate lives. But Belinda was facing a dilemma. After sharing her body with Griffin would she be able to walk away unscathed? Would she become an emotional cripple and not be able to let him go? Or would she revert to the woman who with a single hostile glare was able to keep men at a distance and out of her bed?

"Are you certain you want this?" Griffin asked Belinda. "Are you willing to do this for the next eleven years without asking for more?"

Belinda was too stunned to speak. So she did the next best thing. She nodded. Why would he ask her something like that? She lay in his bed, butt-naked, her body thrumming from a desire only he could assuage, and he wanted to ask her about eleven years from now. No one knew where they'd be the next day, so a decade was more than a stretch.

Reaching for the hem of his T-shirt, Griffin pulled it up and over his head. He felt as if he were in a hypnotic trance—that what was about to happen wasn't actually happening, that he was dreaming and when he awoke he would be in bed—alone. He'd lost count of the women with whom he bedded or dated that had become Belinda Eaton in his fantasies. It took a long time for him to rid himself of the guilt that he was lusting after his sister-in-law, because they didn't share a bloodline. His brother had fallen in love with her sister, and he, in turn, had fallen in love with her.

He smiled at Belinda. "I had to ask."

His hands were steady as he relieved himself of his jeans and boxers in one, smooth motion. He glanced down when he heard Belinda gasp and saw the direction of her gaze. He was aroused. His erection so hard it was painful—exquisite, pleasurable pain.

What Griffin had hoped for wasn't going to happen. He'd wanted making love with Belinda to be slow, but the inferno in his groin threatened to incinerate him. Leaning over, he opened the drawer to the nightstand and took out a condom. His hands shook slightly when he opened the packet and sheathed his tumescence in latex.

They shared a smile when Belinda raised her arms and opened her legs to welcome Griffin Rice not only into her life but also into her body. She'd had years to prepare for something she'd fantasized over and over. Instinctively, her body arched toward him, her arms going around his neck.

She was helpless to halt the gasps and soft moans that slipped past her parted lips when Griffin's rapacious mouth explored the skin on her neck, shoulders, journeying down the length of her body to stake his claim between her thighs. Men had touched her *there,* but none had ever kissed her *there.*

Griffin's tongue searched and found the swollen nub shimmering with moisture, his tongue worshipping the folds between the tangled curls concealing her femininity. Belinda smelled sweet, tasted sweet. The smell of desire became an aphrodisiac that threatened to take him beyond himself. He pushed his face closer while inhaling her essence. Now he knew what men meant when they claimed they wanted to climb inside a woman.

Passion pounded, whirling the blood through Belinda's heart, head and chest. She was mindless with desire for a man she hadn't planned to love, a man whom she'd never let know she loved him.

She was on fire! Griffin's hands and mouth had started a blaze and there was only one way it could be extinguished.

Her hands came down, her fingertips biting into the muscle and sinew covering his shoulders. Her body was throbbing, between her legs was thrumming an ancient rhythm that forced her to move.

"Griffin! Please stop." Her whispered entreaty became a litany of desperation. "Don't torment me."

Griffin pressed a lingering kiss to Belinda's quivering thighs. He couldn't believe she was begging him not to torment her when that's exactly what she'd been doing for thirteen years. Well, he was going to end the torment—for both of them.

He positioned his rigid flesh at the entrance to her femininity. Like a heat-seeking missile locked on its target, he eased his sex into Belinda, registering the gasps against his ear. It was his turn to gasp when the walls of her vagina closed tightly around him, holding him captive in a sensual vise from which he didn't want to escape.

Griffin pushed gently, in and out, setting a strong thrusting rhythm Belinda followed easily.

He pushed.

She pushed back.

He rolled his hips.

She rolled her hips.

Still joined, Griffin went to his knees, slipped his hands under her hips and lifted her legs off the mattress. Together they found a tempo that bound their bodies together, making them one.

Belinda stared up at her lover, awed by the carnal expression on his face as she felt his sex swell, becoming harder and plunging deeper into her once-chaste body. She and Griffin had become man and woman, flesh against flesh. He'd become her lover and she his. The flutters began softly, growing more intense and seeking an escape.

"Griffin!"

She screamed his name in strident desperation, making the hair on the back of Griffin's neck stand up. Heat, followed by chills and another swath of heat shook him from head to toe, finally settling at the base of his spine. He affected a slow, rocking motion that escalated to powerful thrusts punctuated with groans overlapping moans of ecstasy when Belinda and Griffin succumbed to a shared passion and they surrendered all they were to each other.

Collapsing on the slender body beneath him, Griffin waited for his breathing to return to normal at the same time Belinda's breath came in long, surrendering moans. She was exquisite—in and out of bed.

Belinda pushed against Griffin's shoulder in an

attempt to get him to move off her. "Darling, you're crushing me."

Rolling off her, Griffin reversed their positions, sandwiching her legs between his. He smiled up at her moist face. "Am I really your darling?"

She offered him a small, demure smile. "Yes. But that's because I'm your baby."

A soft chuckle rumbled in his broad chest. "That you are."

Belinda sobered quickly. "If we're going to sleep together, then I'm going on the Pill."

"You don't trust me to protect you?"

"It's not about trust, Griffin. It's personal. If I did become pregnant, then it becomes my responsibility."

Griffin didn't have a comeback to her decision to take responsibility for contraception. It was her body, and he had no right to tell her what to do with her body. And, he also wanted Belinda to trust him—with her life and her future.

"Are you sure?" he asked.

Belinda nodded. "I'm very sure. I want to plan for my children. If and when I decide to start a family I'd like to get pregnant in the fall and deliver as close to the summer as possible. Then, I'll have two to three months to bond with my baby before the start of the next school year."

Griffin stared at Belinda in disbelief. She was more anal that he'd originally thought. "What happens if you don't get pregnant in the fall?"

"I'll wait and try again the following year."

He wanted to tell her that her view of family planning was asinine but didn't want to say anything to jeopardize the fact that they'd taken their relationship to another level. Asinine or not, he loved Belinda, enough to agree to almost anything and everything she wanted.

Belinda moved off Griffin's body and lay beside him. Turning on her side, she settled back against him, enjoying the feel of his arm around her as she pressed her hips to his groin and they lay like two spoons. The slight ache between her legs was a reminder of certain muscles she hadn't used in a long time. She emitted a soft sigh as she closed her eyes and shifted into a more comfortable position.

"Are you all right?" Griffin's breath swept over the nape of her neck.

Belinda frowned. "I'm good. I'm really good."

"No flashbacks from yesterday?"

Griffin hadn't broached the subject of the school shooting because he wanted Belinda to open up to him on her own. But she hadn't, and he feared she'd suppressed the horrific incident. He wanted and needed her to talk about it before their charges returned home. If Belinda had a meltdown in front of the girls, he feared it would prove damaging to their continuing emotional healing.

"No. That's not to say I won't have nightmares later on."

"Do you plan to talk to a counselor?"

"I don't know. I'm praying I don't lose it when classes resume."

"I think you should consider seeing a counselor."

"I don't need one when I have you. I've revealed things to you about my past that I've never told anyone. And I'm counting on attorney-client privilege that you won't repeat it."

Griffin laughed. "What goes on in the bedroom stays in the bedroom."

There came a prolonged silence, as Belinda mentally

relived the two hours before the police negotiator was able to defuse what could've been a massacre if the student had panicked.

"I was more afraid for the kid with the gun than for myself and the other students," she said in a soft voice that Griffin had to strain to hear. "He had become a victim in a situation not of his choosing."

"Why would you say that?"

"He's what I call an outsider. He doesn't fit in with the nerds or with the jocks. He was taken in by a boy who wanted him to shoot a female student because she wanted nothing more to do with him."

"If your school has metal detectors, then how did he get the gun past the security checkpoint?"

"Someone passed it to him through the window. He must have lost his nerve because he fired shots at the ceiling and windows rather than at his intended target. After I called 911, I tried to convince him to throw the gun out the window. He started crying and fired off another round. We lay on the floor under desks until a SWAT team surrounded the school building and a police negotiator called the classroom and tried to convince him to release his hostages."

"How did it end?" Griffin asked.

"He gave up his friend who'd set up the hit, then asked to speak to his mother. I don't know what she said to him, but he removed the clip from the gun and tossed both out the window. The police stormed the classroom like marines hitting a beach, and that was more trauma-tizing than someone with a gun who hadn't the nerve to step on a bug. I hope wherever he winds up that he'll get some help."

Griffin splayed his fingers over her belly. "Let's hope

his parents can convince a judge that he's not a criminal, but a troubled youth."

Turning over, Belinda stared at her lover. "He's a good kid, and one of my best students. His mother is a single mother with five kids who works two jobs to keep her family together. Do you think you can—"

Griffin stopped her when he put his hand over her mouth. "No, baby, I will not take on his case. I'm shaky at best when it comes to criminal law. What I'll do is call a friend who'll occasionally take pro bono cases to see if the boy has been appointed a public defender."

Belinda trailed her fingers down Griffin's smooth chest to his belly and still lower to the flaccid flesh between his muscular thighs. "Thank you, darling."

Griffin felt his sex harden quickly when Belinda caressed him in an up-and-down motion. A swath of desire left him gasping as he struggled to force air into his lungs. Her hands and fingers worked their magic, squeezing and manipulating his erection until he feared spilling his passion on the sheets.

Somewhere between the vestiges of sanity and insanity, he managed to extract her hand, slip on protection and entered Belinda in one, sure thrust of his hips. He rode her fast, hard and when they reversed positions Belinda, bracing her hands on his chest and thighs, took him to heights of passion he'd glimpsed but never experienced. It ended when they collapsed to the moist sheets, both struggling to breathe.

Belinda stared at Griffin through half-lowered lids when he slipped off the bed to discard the condoms. She went into Griffin's outstretched arms when he returned. They lay together, limbs entwined, and fell asleep.

Chapter 10

Belinda avoided watching television because she didn't want to be reminded of the incident at her high school. Her mother had called to say reporters had come by when they were informed that the teacher whose classroom was under siege was the daughter of Dr. Dwight Eaton.

Belinda, sitting on a high stool in Griffin's kitchen, rolled her eyes even though Roberta couldn't see her. "Mama, why is the media trying to turn this into a Columbine? And what the hell are they talking about when they said the school was under siege? I'm not attempting to minimize what happened but shouldn't everyone be happy that no one was killed?"

"Bullets and carnage sell newspapers and commercial airtime, not feel-good stories. You should know that, Lindy."

"I do, Mama."

"If you do, then you should know the entire country is looking at us, because most of the school shootings have been in rural areas, not a major urban city like Philly. What I'm afraid of is copycat idiots who want either their names in the paper or are looking for martyrdom. It seems as if there're more fools out here than sensible folk."

"I think you're right."

"I know I'm right, Lindy. Now, how are you getting along with Griffin?"

"We're good."

"I didn't ask about Griffin. I asked about you, Belinda Jacqueline Eaton."

Belinda took in a quick breath. It wasn't often her mother called her by her given name, and it was even rarer when she referred to her by her full name. "I'm getting along very well with him, thank you very much. In fact, we're going out to dinner tonight."

"I've always liked Griffin. It always struck me as odd why he hasn't settled down."

"Maybe you should ask him the next time you see him, Roberta Alice Stewart-Eaton."

A soft laugh came through the earpiece of Belinda's cell phone. "Of all my children you were always the most vocal one, Lindy."

"Didn't you raise your daughters to speak their minds?"

"Yes, I did. Outspoken or not, I'd like to see you married so you can give me a few more grandchildren."

"It's not going to happen, Mama, until Sabrina and Layla turn twenty-three."

"Twenty-three is not a magic number, Lindy. Things will begin to change next year when the girls turn thirteen

and become young adults. Staying home with their mom
and dad playing Scrabble or Uno will no longer hold their
interest. It'll be the mall, movies, the beach and sleep-
overs. You'll have to make an appointment just to see
them once they start driving. After that it'll be college,
football games, fiancés and marriage. And where will
you be? Sitting home waiting for someone to knock on
the door to tell you that he's the man you've spent your
life waiting for? I don't think so, Belinda."

Belinda couldn't stop the smile spreading across her
face. "I get your point, Mama."

"If that's the case, then I'm going to hang up because
my man is waiting to take me away for the weekend."
Roberta had cancelled Sunday dinner because her
granddaughters were away.

"Have fun, Mama, and tell Daddy if he can't be good,
then he should be careful."

"I will," Roberta said, laughing. "Enjoy your night out."

"Thank you. Enjoy your weekend."

Belinda ended the call and slipped off the stool. She
went still when she saw Griffin standing at the entrance to
the kitchen. How long had he been there, and how much
of the conversation with her mother had he overheard?

She flashed a brittle smile. "I'm ready."

Griffin approached Belinda, his dark gaze unreadable.
They'd spent the past three days "playing house." They
slept and took turns cooking. He'd returned to Philly to
finalize the relocation of GR Sports Enterprises, Limited.
All of the files were in cartons and labeled with their
contents. He'd contracted with a bonded moving company,
and the cartons were delivered earlier that morning. Griffin
knew he had to go through every sheet of paper to ascer-
tain what he would keep and what would be shredded.

Unlike many sports attorneys and agents his client list was limited to six. It was a number he could manage without taking on a partner, and it permitted him the option of being very selective. There were athletes who'd solicited him to represent them and he'd turned them down—some because of a history of substance abuse or run-ins with the law, or those who wanted him to become a miracle worker when they requested astronomical salaries that were out of line. His baseball-attendance clause was legendary. If a ballplayer put fans in stadium seats, then they were guaranteed a share of the profits. He'd done well for his clients, and the money he earned from negotiating their contracts and endorsements afforded him a very comfortable lifestyle.

"You look very chic."

Belinda nodded. "Thank you."

When Griffin informed her that he'd made dinner reservations at Barclay Prime, a popular steak house in Rittenhouse, the former neighborhood of Philadelphia's blue bloods, she'd decided to wear a tailored light gray wool gabardine suit with a darker gray silk blouse. Her accessories were a single strand of pearls and matching studs in her pierced lobes. Griffin was drop-dead gorgeous in a chocolate-brown suit, white shirt and checked tie.

He winked at Belinda. She wore the straighter, sleek hairstyle he favored because it made her appear more sophisticated, womanly. Whenever she affected the curly style her personality reflected her more playful side.

Reaching for her hand, Griffin brought it to his lips, kissing her fingers before he tucked it into the bend of his elbow. "We have to leave now." He'd had to work a minor miracle to secure a reservation on such short notice. He'd become a regular customer since he dined there with his clients, their friends and family members.

Leaning into him, Belinda rested her forehead against his ear. "I have something to tell you," she whispered cryptically.

Griffin froze. Was she going to tell him what he'd been waiting to hear? Each time they made love he had to bite down on his lower lip to keep from blurting out that he'd fallen in love with her.

He gave her a sidelong look. "What is it?"

A mysterious smile played at the corners of her mouth. "I could very easily get used to playing house with you."

Griffin couldn't help smiling. It wasn't what he wanted to hear, but it was close enough. "I'm very happy to know that."

Belinda blinked once. "Do we have to stay in character while in public?"

His smile faded. "What are you talking about?"

"We're going out together and how do you want me to relate to you? Am I a friend or something more?"

"We are what we are."

"And what's that, Griffin?"

He glared at her. "We are lovers," Griffin spat out, enunciating each word.

We are lovers. The three words stayed with Belinda during the drive from Paoli and into Philadelphia, while Griffin parked his sport-utility vehicle in a garage on Chancellor Street, and it reminded her of their status when she and her *lover* were seated in the lounge waiting for a table.

Griffin caressed her hair, smoothing wayward strands clinging to her cheek. "Have you ever dined here?"

It hadn't surprised Belinda that Griffin was on first-name basis with the maître d' and waitstaff. She stared at a spot over his shoulder, refusing to look directly at him and still smarting from his brusque response to her query as to their status. It was Griffin who was the cause célèbre whom paparazzi photographed with actresses, models or recording artists.

Fortunately for her, her fifteen minutes of fame was thwarted by the school superintendent's refusal to disclose or verify the names of his teachers or students to the press, leading Belinda to believe it was a student or a parent who'd leaked her name.

"No. This is my first time."

Resting an arm on the bar, Griffin stared at Belinda's tight expression. "I'm sorry."

"For what, Griffin?" Belinda decided she wasn't going to make it easy for him. She wasn't going to establish a precedence of having him snap at her, only to apologize later when he didn't have to use the tone from the onset.

"I'm sorry for the way I spoke to you. I had no right—"

"You better believe you had no right," she countered. "I told you before I'll not be talked down to or yelled at. Why is that so difficult for you to grasp?"

"Dammit, Belinda! I said I was sorry. What do you want me to do, get on my knees?"

Pursing her mouth and appearing deep in thought, Belinda gave him a direct stare. The sooty shadow on her eyelids made her eyes look seductive and mysterious. "No, Griffin. I don't want you to crawl. It wouldn't be good for your image."

"What image?"

"Griff, darling. Is that you?"

Belinda and Griffin turned at the same time to see a woman in a stretch-knit black dress that was at least two sizes too small for her voluptuous body. Her balance was compromised by four-inch stilettos, a platinum wig circa 1760 and breast augmentation; layers of nut-brown pancake makeup failed to conceal an outbreak of adult acne.

Griffin moved off his stool, frowning. He loathed having to acknowledge a woman he wanted to forget. "Hello, Deanna. How are you?"

"It's all good, handsome." Light brown eyes framed by thick black false lashes focused on the woman with Griffin Rice. "How long has it been, Griff?"

"It has to be a couple of years."

"Try three," Deanna drawled. "You're forgetting your manners, darling. Aren't you going to introduce me to your *little date?*"

Wrapping an arm around Belinda's waist, Griffin moved behind her stool. "Belinda, this is Deanna…"

"Monique," Deanna supplied. "Remember you used to joke about me having two first names?"

Griffin's expression was impassive. "Belinda, this is Deanna Monique," he began again as if Deanna hadn't interrupted him. "Deanna, this is Belinda Eaton."

Deanna waved her left hand and light caught the fire of a large diamond solitaire on her ring finger. Belinda found it difficult to pinpoint the woman's age, so she estimated somewhere between thirty-five and forty. She thought her cute in a Kewpie doll sort of way.

"It's nice meeting you, Deanna."

Deanna waved her hand again. "Let me give you a little piece of advice where it concerns Griff Rice. If you're hoping to get married, then you're with the wrong man."

Belinda didn't like people who kiss and tell, and apparently Deanna either wanted to make her aware that she'd dated Griffin, or it was a case of sour grapes because he'd refused to marry her.

Griffin's arm tightened around Belinda's waist. "In case you're not familiar with the name, baby, Deanna Monique is a columnist who writes for a supermarket tabloid."

Peering up over her shoulder, Belinda made an attractive moue. "I never read them."

A waiter came over to Deanna. "Miss Monique, your table is ready. Will you kindly follow me." Waving to Griffin and Belinda, the reporter followed the waiter, tiptoeing as if she were walking on ice.

"She's quite a character," Belinda said after she'd disappeared from view.

Griffin signaled to the bartender. "That she is," he remarked, retaking his stool. "Eccentric but harmless. I'm going to order a martini. Would you like something?"

"I'll have an apple martini."

The bartender had just served their drinks when a waiter informed them that their table was ready. Belinda felt the way Deanna appeared, as she attempted to maintain her balance while she carried her cocktail to the table without spilling it. She placed the glass on the table and thanked Griffin when he seated her. Their waiter handed them menus, then stood a short distance away, waiting for them to select their entrées.

She glanced around the dining room. "This is very nice, Griffin." The ground floor of a Rittenhouse Square apartment building had been transformed into a restaurant resembling a library with elegant crystal chandeliers, marble tables and walnut bookcases.

Reaching for his glass, he extended it, and he wasn't disappointed when Belinda raised her glass and touched his. "Here's to the woman who makes me appreciate being a man."

Her face burned as she recalled what had passed between them earlier that morning. They'd been insatiable—making love, sleeping and waking up to make love again. "Same here. But, of course, being a woman."

Belinda took a sip of the icy concoction, finding it delicious. The chill warmed and spread to her chest and lower, to the nether portions of her body. By the time she'd had her second sip she'd forgotten her former annoyance with Griffin and settled back in her chair to enjoy her drink and the man whom she loved with every fiber of her being.

"That is the best steak I've ever eaten." Belinda had ordered the Australian Tajima Kobe filet that literally melted on her tongue.

Griffin smiled. "Eating here will turn a hard-core vegetarian into a carnivore."

"Shame on you," she chided softly, smiling.

"It made a believer of me."

Her fork halted midair. "You were a vegetarian." Her query came out as a statement.

Dabbing his mouth with a napkin, Griffin angled his head. "There was one time when I flirted with the notion of becoming a vegetarian. I'd given up beef and chicken, eating only fish, veggies and fruit."

"That's sacrilegious, Griffin."

"Why is it sacrilegious?"

"It would mean giving up a Geno's Philly cheesesteak."

"That's easy. Now, if you'd said Pat's King of Steaks I'd have to agree with you."

Belinda placed a hand over her chest and pretended to swoon. The mellowing effects of martini had kicked in. "What! You prefer Pat's to Geno's?"

"It's been documented that Pat outsells Geno twelve-to-one."

"I beg to differ with you, counselor. It just appears that way because if ten people crowd into Geno's, it's packed. But twenty-five or even thirty can fit into Pat's with room to spare."

Griffin and Belinda continued the good-natured debate over who made the best Philly cheesesteak over a dinner of premium aged beef, truffle-whipped potatoes, asparagus and shared a Barclay salad for two. Both agreed that substituting pork or chicken for beef was truly a crime.

Reaching across the table, Belinda rested a hand atop Griffin's. "It's still not too late to convert to vegetarianism. I've heard there is a veggie cheesesteak."

"How can a steak not be meat? And is there such a word as *vegetarianism*?"

She managed to look insulted. "Of course there's such a word. After all, I am a teacher."

"A history teacher, Miss Eaton," Griffin reminded her.

"Oh. Are you implying that history teachers don't read, Mr. Rice?"

"They know dates and historical facts."

"We also read," she insisted, smiling.

"I'm going to give you a pop history quiz."

"Let's hear, counselor."

Griffin's eyes glittered with merriment. "Who were the candidates in the…" He hesitated. Presidential elections were always held during a leap year. "Who were the candidates in the eighteen seventy-six presidential election?"

Belinda wanted to tell her lover that he'd walked into a trap of his own choosing. She knew the details of every election from Washington to the sitting president.

"Republican Governor Rutherford B. Hayes of Ohio ran against New York Democratic Governor Samuel J. Tilden, who won a majority of the popular vote, but was one electoral vote short of a necessary majority, while Hayes was twenty votes short."

"Tilden had more votes, yet Hayes became President?"

Belinda stared at Griffin, wondering how much he knew about the centennial election. "Yes. Charges arose of irregularities concerning vote-counting procedures in three Southern states: Louisiana, South Carolina and Florida where the election boards were under the control of Reconstruction-era Republicans."

Belinda's intelligence never ceased to amaze Griffin. She was very smart and she knew it. It was why she came back at him whenever she felt he was talking down to her. "I know Hayes was sworn in as president, but how did he pull it off being down twenty votes?"

"After the election board count indicated these three states had given Hayes the majority, Democrats charged the vote in each state actually went to Tilden, which would've given Tilden the victory. The three states sent two sets of returns to Congress, one to the Democrats and one to the Republicans.

"Congress then established a fifteen-member electoral commission—the Electoral Count Act—to resolve what had become an unprecedented constitutional crisis. After a lot of rhetoric, the commission members agreed to accept the Republican returns, giving Hayes a one-vote electoral victory. The two parties decided to play nice with each other when the Democrats agreed

Hayes would take office in return for withdrawing federal troops from the last two remaining states—Louisiana and South Carolina. The action officially ended military Reconstruction in the South. Most people are unaware the two thousand election wasn't the first time questions as to voting irregularities had become a national issue."

"It looks as if our election process hasn't come that far in one hundred twenty-four years."

Belinda wrinkled her nose. "It's called *poli-tricks*."

Griffin stared at her and then burst out laughing. "Speaking of poli-tricks, I have tickets to a fund-raiser for a local politician next month, and I'd like you to come with me."

"Will it be a date?" she teased.

"Of course it is. Don't you know when you're being courted, Miss Eaton?"

A cautionary voice whispered in her head that Griffin was changing the rules of their relationship. To her, courting meant a social interaction that led to an engagement and marriage.

It was apparent he was sending mixed signals. "No, I didn't."

"Well, consider yourself warned."

She stared at him with complete surprise etched on her face. The seconds ticked off, then she said, "Point taken."

Chapter 11

Griffin peered over Belinda's shoulder as she gathered the ingredients for Sunday dinner. Not wanting to break a family tradition, she'd offered to cook rather than go out or order in.

"What are you going to do with Bruiser?" A large whole chicken rested on a cutting board.

Belinda smiled up at Griffin. "I'm going to put garlic butter under the skin, stuff the cavity with carrots, potatoes and shallots and cook it in a roasting bag."

He took a step and grasped the chicken's wings, lifting it in the air. "Hey, dude, you look as if you've pumped a little iron. Lindy, look at the thighs on this sucker."

"Griffin! Put that bird down. I just washed it."

"You think you can take me?" he asked the roaster, shaking it from side to side. "No? What are you? Are you chicken? You're not a chicken. You're a punk," Griffin said, continuing his monologue with the bird. He gave the roaster a final shake. "Tell me now. Who's ya daddy?"

Belinda couldn't help herself doubling over in laughter. The sight of Griffin Rice challenging a chicken to a fight was priceless. She was laughing so hard that tears rolled down her face.

"Stop it," she ordered, hiccuping while trying to catch her breath.

Griffin tossed the chicken on the board. "You're an embarrassment to the poultry community. I wash my hands of you." Using his elbow, he activated the long-handled faucet in one of the two stainless-steel sinks, washing and rinsing his hands.

Belinda handed him a paper towel. "You know you're a very sick man."

"Why would you say that?"

"You were talking to a chicken, Griffin. A dead chicken."

"Nigel and Cecil refuse to play with me, so Chicken Big was next."

She shook her head in amazement. Griffin was a bigger kid than his nieces. "Why won't they play with you?" He'd gotten up early to clean the cage and give the pups fresh food and clean water.

"I don't know. When I opened the cage door they just sat there looking at me. And when I reached in to take them out Nigel tried to bite me, while Cecil started growling and showing his teeth."

"You can't deal with two three-pound puppies, so you decide to take your frustration out on a chicken— or should I say our dinner."

Resting his hands on Belinda's shoulders, Griffin kissed the nape of her neck. "I'm sorry about abusing Bruiser."

"An idle mind is the devil's workshop. Perhaps I should put you to work…"

"What do you want me to do?"

She glanced up at him. "I need for you to make garlic butter."

He brushed a kiss over her lips. "Yummy."

"Sweet," Belinda crooned, deepening the kiss.

Griffin enjoyed cooking with Belinda. He wasn't a novice when it came to food. Most of his dishes were simple and palatable. However, Belinda would add the pièce de résistance with exotic seasonings and presentation.

He had to admit they worked well together—in and out of bed. They didn't agree on everything, and he still found her rigid and unrelenting when it came to some child-rearing issues. Griffin attributed that not so much to her upbringing as to her career as a teacher. Ten years of teaching young adults was challenging. Teaching young adults in one of Philadelphia's most challenging high schools was not only demanding, but difficult.

After the classroom shooting incident he'd broached the subject with Belinda of possibly transferring to another high school, one that was less violent. She'd calmly replied, "When I want or need your advice I'll ask for it." It was a not-so-subtle way of her telling him to mind his own business.

What Belinda needed to understand was that she was as much his business as Sabrina and Layla, and he was as much her business as her nieces. The four of them were inexorably linked by blood and marriage. His bloodline and Belinda's would continue with their nieces and that meant they were family.

Griffin inserted a clove of garlic in a garlic press. The

fragrant and distinctive aroma filled the kitchen. He added it to the dish of butter that had been left to soften to room temperature. "Is one clove enough?" he asked.

Belinda stopped peeling carrots. "It could use another one. Don't blend it yet. I want to add a few sprigs of fresh chopped parsley. Who taught you to cook?" she asked Griffin when he chopped parsley as if he were a professional chef.

"I had a girlfriend who was a chef," Griffin admitted reluctantly. He didn't want to talk about a woman or the women in his past. The soothing sound of music coming from a built-in radio under the kitchen cabinet punctuated the silence that ensued.

Belinda smiled as she sprinkled coarse sea salt on small redskin potatoes. "Lucky you."

His head came up as he stared numbly at her. "Why would you say that?"

"You don't have to rely on a woman to cook for you. Do you know how many men hook up with women because they're looking for someone to feed them?"

"That's a lot of bull, Lindy. They could always pay someone in the neighborhood to cook meals for them. They hook up with women because some of them are parasites. There's a guy I know who refused to commit to one woman because he said he needed variety. There was Sandra, who was always willing to cook, whenever he dropped by for breakfast, lunch or dinner. Then he had Jackie because she did everything he wanted her to do in bed. And then there was Melissa, his baby mama, who opened her door to him even if he stayed away for months because she claimed she wanted her son to have a relationship with his father."

"That's ridiculous, Griffin. A child can't bond with

a parent when he or she sees them only two or three times a year."

"That's what I'd tell Jerrold, but anything I said fell on deaf ears. Although my parents lived under the same roof, my dad's cheating not only affected my mother but Grant and me."

Belinda gave Griffin a sidelong glance. His expression was one she'd never seen before. It was obvious his father's infidelity had scarred him. "I don't believe Grant ever cheated on my sister."

"That's because he couldn't cheat, not after hearing my mother argue with Dad because he'd come home with the scent of another woman still on him. Grant used to put his hands over his ears to shut out their shouting at each other."

"What did you do, Griffin?"

"I sat on the back porch until Dad left. It didn't matter how late he stayed out screwing other women, he always came home and he always went to work."

"Why didn't your mother leave him?"

Griffin's motions were slow, methodical as he folded the chopped parsley and minced garlic into the softened butter. "Her father died when she was a little girl, so she said she didn't want her children to grow up without their father."

"But your father cheated on her."

"Yes, he did. And the ultimate indignity was that he didn't try to hide it."

"Why do men cheat?"

Griffin's eyes caught and held hers. "Why do women cheat?"

"They don't cheat as much as men."

"Are you certain about that statistic? Didn't Oprah

have a segment about women who admitted to cheating? That the percentage of women who cheat is a lot higher than most people believe, so let's not get into comparing genders."

"I didn't ask the question for you to answer with another question." Belinda's voice was low and soft.

The seconds ticked away as they regarded each other. "I wouldn't know, Lindy, because I've never cheated on a woman. Even if I thought about it I don't think I would cheat because I saw what it did to my mother and how it affected Grant and me. Instead of being children and enjoying the things little boys did, we were drawn into a battle that involved marital problems. Six- and nine-year-olds shouldn't have to hear words like *pussy* and *dick* thrown around like *please* and *thank you*—especially from their parents."

"Even though she didn't grow up with her father, your mother didn't have to stay, especially when you and Grant were older."

"That was something Grant and I asked her, and her response was that she loved her cheating husband. That was something I couldn't wrap my head around until Gloria Bailey-Rice told me about the man she'd fallen in love with, who was not the one he'd become."

Belinda knew she would never stay with a man who she knew was cheating on her. When she'd discovered the teacher she was dating was also dating another colleague she ended the relationship before he could open his mouth to explain.

"Why did she finally divorce your father?"

Inhaling, Griffin held his breath and then let it out slowly. "She didn't divorce him. He divorced her."

"But… But why? Why would he leave, Griffin?"

Belinda stuttered. "He had the best of both worlds—a married man with a family behaving as if he were single."

"Grant and I threatened him." Griffin recognized shock and another unidentifiable emotion in Belinda's eyes when she met his gaze. "I was a junior in high school when Grant came home from college during a school break and we sat down together to discuss our parents' marriage. Nothing had changed in more than twenty years. My dad was still sleeping with other women, and my mother was still fighting about something she couldn't change or control.

"She'd become an insomniac. She stayed up half the night, hoping to witness the time he came home. I had no idea what she was going to do with that information except to use it if or when she decided to divorce him. And, even worse, she'd begun following him and confronting his women.

"I told my brother we were going to lose our mother to an emotional breakdown or she was going to confront the wrong woman and end up dead. We set up a private meeting with Dad and told him that if he didn't move out of the house we were going to kick his ass and throw him out. To this day I couldn't say for sure whether I would've actually hit my father. Thankfully I didn't have to be put to the test."

"How soon after did he leave?"

"It took him a week to get up the nerve to tell his wife he was leaving and filing for divorce."

"What was your mother's reaction?"

Griffin flashed a devastatingly sensual smile. "She went to a spa in Sedona, Arizona, for two weeks and came back with a new look and new attitude. She occasionally goes out with other men, but she vowed never to marry again."

"Don't you think it's odd that your mom and dad went away together for a month?"

"Not really," Griffin said, shaking his head. "Mom could care less who her ex-husband sleeps with, and because she'd doesn't care, Dad knows he has no power over her."

Belinda smiled. "Would you like for them to reconcile?"

"Maybe I'm selfish, but no. There's more respect between them now than there ever was when they were together."

"Your father is wonderful with his granddaughters."

"That's because he spoils them."

And, you don't, Belinda thought, giving Griffin a knowing smile.

He moved closer, trapping her body between his and the countertop. "What's that look all about?" he whispered near her ear.

"What look?" said she innocently.

Griffin pressed closer, his groin pressed to her hips. "The one that said I'm also culpable."

"Do you really think you know me so well that you can read my mind?"

Lowering his head he fastened his mouth to the nape of her neck, smiling when he felt a faint shudder go through Belinda. "I can't read your mind, but I can read your expressions. Your face is like an open book. You'd never make it as a poker player because everyone would know when you're not bluffing."

"It doesn't matter because I don't gamble."

"You've never gambled on anything in your life?" he asked, trailing a series of light kisses down the column of her long, scented neck.

Belinda smothered a gasp when she felt her knees weaken as his mouth searched the flesh bared by her tank top. "Griffin, stop or we're not going to eat tonight."

Griffin's hands were busy searching under her top. "Speak for yourself, Lindy. I plan to eat even if Bruiser never makes it into the oven."

It took a full minute before she realized Griffin wasn't talking about food. "I happen to like my meat well done."

"And I like a little pink in mine," Griffin countered.

She bit back a smile. "You are *so* nasty, Griffin Rice."

"So are you, Lindy Eaton, or you wouldn't have known what I was talking about."

Belinda managed to make Griffin take a step back when she elbowed him in the ribs. Shifting, she gave him a direct stare. "I wasn't nasty before I hooked up with you."

"Am I to take credit for unleashing the nastiness?"

She affected a moue, bringing his gaze to linger on her mouth. "Only some of it."

Griffin lifted his expressive eyebrows. "Are you saying that there's more?"

Pressing her breasts to his chest, Belinda went on tiptoe. "There's so much more, lover. You've only begun to scratch the surface."

Crushing her to his length, his lips descended slowly to meet hers, drinking in the sweetness of her kiss. Deepening the kiss and forcing her lips apart with his thrusting tongue, Griffin wanted to devour Belinda where they stood.

He wanted to take her on the kitchen floor. Now he understood animals in heat whose sole intent was to mate. And that's what he wanted to do with Belinda. He wanted to mate with her again and again to guarantee that his gene pool would continue. All he thought of was ripping her clothes from her curvy, lithe body and taking her without a pretense of foreplay, but the revelation of her near-rape stopped his traitorous musings. What he didn't want to do was trigger a flashback of the traumatic episode.

The kiss ended as quickly as it'd begun. Belinda took a step backward, her chest rising and falling as if she'd run a race. She glanced away. "I have to finish preparing dinner." Her voice was a whisper.

"I'll be in the back," Griffin said as he spun on his heels and walked out of the kitchen.

Belinda's hands were shaking uncontrollably from the build-up of sexual tension that lingered like waves of heat. She knew she'd been as close to losing control as Griffin. It seemed as if every time they came together the encounter was more passionate and explosive than the one that preceded it.

If Griffin hadn't stopped when he did she would've begged him to make love to her in the kitchen, without protection and when it was the most fertile time in her cycle. She'd called her gynecologist and asked that he call in a prescription to her local pharmacist for a supply of birth control pills that she would pick up the following day. She informed Griffin that he would have to continue to use protection until she went back on the Pill. They'd agreed to play house, but having a baby was not a part of the agreement.

Belinda sat staring at the same page in the book that lay on her lap, seeing but not reading any of the words. This was to become her last night in Paoli that she and Griffin would share a bed. The bus carrying Sabrina, Layla and their classmates from Gettysburg was scheduled to arrive at the school around three the following afternoon.

A moving company had delivered cartons of files from Griffin's Philadelphia office to the one he'd set up in his home, and the woman he'd hired as a part-time secretary/paralegal spent three full days conferring with him while she set up a filing system.

Belinda left Griffin a note, telling him that she was taking his car to go to her post office to pick up the mail they were holding for her. She also stopped at the pharmacy to pick up the three-month supply of low-dose birth control pills. She visited briefly with her mother, who'd insisted on making lunch for the two of them. Roberta hadn't asked about Griffin, which led her to believe that she knew they were sleeping together. It'd taken her a while to come to the conclusion that mothers knew more about their children than they let on. She returned to Paoli to discover Griffin had prepared a dinner of roast salmon with basil and sweet pepper sauce and a salad.

Griffin had suggested going for a walk after dinner and when strolling the quiet tree-lined streets holding hands she felt as if she'd stepped back in time when her father had given her permission to date. Most times she and her boyfriend sat on the porch, or if they left the porch it was to walk around the neighborhood under the watchful eyes of neighbors who were more than willing to report anything that appeared inappropriate to the elder Eatons.

"When are you going to turn the page?" asked a deep voice behind her.

Belinda closed the novel, stood up and turned to find Griffin standing less than three feet away; she wondered why she hadn't heard his approach. "I guess I was daydreaming."

Griffin stared at the woman who'd become an integral part of his life. It'd been raining off and on for two days and while the weather hadn't affected him because he'd been busy setting up his home office, it'd played havoc with her nerves.

She complained she wasn't used to sitting around doing nothing, which if she'd been home she'd keep busy doing housework, doing laundry or grocery shopping. It was different in Paoli because a cleaning service kept the house spotless and a landscaping company maintained the yard. Griffin shopped for groceries every other month, with the exception of perishables, at a supermarket warehouse, buying in bulk and storing it in the finished basement.

Belinda had changed in front of his eyes. Her body appeared more rounded, which she attributed to eating three meals a day. Sitting outside on the patio during daylight hours had darkened her face to a rich sable-brown. And with her scrubbed face, hair secured in an elastic band, faded jeans and oversize T-shirt she could easily pass for one of her students.

They'd played house for eight days and it would end in less than twenty-four hours when they picked up their nieces.

"Good or bad?"

Belinda smiled. "Daydreams are always good. It's the nightmares that are bad."

Griffin angled his head. "Do you ever have nightmares?"

Her eyelids fluttered wildly. "I used to."

He closed the distance between them, his hands

sliding down her arms and tightening around her waist. "I'm glad they're gone."

There was something in Griffin's voice, the way he was touching her that made Belinda want to weep—not in sorrow but in joy.

She loved him.

She'd fallen in love with her sister's brother-in-law, her nieces' uncle, godfather, legal guardian and surrogate father. What had begun as a teenage crush was now full-blown passion with no beginning or end.

Burying her face against his strong, warm brown throat, she closed her eyes. "Love me, darling. Please make love to me for the last time."

"It's not going to be the last time, Lindy."

"Surely you're kidding, Rice. I'm not going to knock boots with you while the girls are in the house."

Attractive lines fanned out around his eyes when he smiled. "Are you afraid they'll hear you screaming in the throes of passion?"

Belinda gave him a soft punch in the middle of his back. "So, you got jokes. At least I don't sound like a bull. You make more noise than I do when you're—"

"Don't say it, baby," Griffin warned. He tightened his hold on her waist. "I get the whole picture—sound and visuals." Bending slightly, he swept her up and into his arms. "Let's go make some noise."

Giggling like a little girl, Belinda tightened her hold around his neck. "How nasty do you want me to be?" she teased.

Throwing back his head, Griffin laughed loudly. "I want you to crank that nasty meter to the highest setting."

She caught his earlobe between her teeth, nipping it gently. "I hope you'll be able to handle it."

"Don't worry about me. Just serve it."

Belinda stared at the slight indentation in his strong chin before her searching gaze moved up to meet his resolute stare. "I'm going to make you scream like a bitch."

"Don't you mean a bull?"

"No-o-o," she drawled with so much attitude that Griffin bit down on his lower lip to keep from smiling.

She tucked her face into the hollow between his neck and shoulder as he left the porch. "Let's take a shower together," Belinda suggested as Griffin entered his bedroom.

Griffin did not drop his gaze as he lowered Belinda until her feet touched the sisal rug under his feet. He undressed her then stood with his arms at his sides while she undressed him, their chests rising and falling in a syncopated rhythm.

Belinda closed her eyes, her breath quickening when his fingers grazed the outline of her breasts. She opened her eyes and smiled. Resting a hand on Griffin's chest, she ran her fingertips over his clavicle, the muscles in his shoulder and lower to his breastbone.

He gasped audibly when her fingers grasped his sex, holding him fast. He hardened almost instantaneously. "Come with me." Like an obedient child, Griffin let Belinda lead him into the adjoining bathroom and shower stall, she still holding on to his erection. "Don't move, darling."

Griffin wanted to tell her he couldn't move even if his life was in the balance. He gasped when she touched a preset dial and lukewarm water flowed down on their heads. Going on tiptoe, she slipped her tongue into his mouth, while her hands worked their magic. Then, without warning, she slid down the length of his body, her mouth replacing her hand. He'd asked Belinda to crank the nasty meter up to its highest setting, demanding that she serve it and that's exactly what she'd done.

Bracing his palms against the tiles, he closed his eyes and tried thinking of something—anything but the image of Belinda on her knees, his sex moving in and out her hot mouth. Heat, chills and then more heat overlapped the iciness snaking its way up his legs and settling at the base of his spine. A groan slipped through his lips when his knees buckled and involuntary tremors had him shaking like a fragile leaf in a strong wind. The muscles in his belly contracted violently when a moan of helplessness, coming from deep within his chest, exploded. He threw back his head and opened his mouth and bellowed.

Belinda didn't make love to Griffin. She commanded him with a raw act of possession, branding him with an indelible mark. He was hers and hers alone. Griffin had taken himself out of circulation and she would make certain he would forget every woman he'd ever known. She was relentless, using her hand, tongue and teeth to bring him to the brink of release. Then without warning, she pressed the pad of her thumb against the large vein behind the shaft, manually slowing down the headlong rush of desire to climax.

Griffin's hands moved with lightning speed when he bent over, anchoring his hands under Belinda's armpits and pulling her to her feet while forcing her to release his engorged flesh. Supporting her back, he lifted her high in the air.

Belinda's small cry of shock was smothered when Griffin covered her mouth with a savage kiss that sucked the oxygen from her lungs. She barely had time to react to the rawness of his sexual onslaught when she found herself on her back and he inside her. Moaning aloud in erotic pleasure, she reveled in the sensation of bare flesh fusing. It was the first time they'd made love without the barrier of latex. Her menses, though scant, had come and gone.

The sensations of falling water, the feel of the coarse hair on his legs against her smooth ones and the unrestrained groans near her ear roused Belinda to a peak of desire bordering on hysteria. Passion radiated from her core, spreading outward to her extremities and beyond.

The turbulence of Griffin's lovemaking hurtled her into a vortex of the sweetest ecstasy. Belinda screamed when she felt him touch her womb and love flowed like heated honey, and she soared higher and higher until she climaxed, experiencing free fall, as Griffin, for the first time, succumbed to *le petit mort.* She couldn't move, didn't want to move as she lay drowning in the lingering aftermath of pure, explosive pleasure.

Griffin recovered before Belinda, coming to his feet. Walking on shaky legs, he reached over and turned off the water. A smile tipped the corners of his mouth when he shifted and saw that Belinda had curled into a fetal position. He hunkered down and eased her off the tiled floor.

Her spiked lashes fluttered when she opened her eyes. "Was I nasty enough for you?"

Shaking his head in amazement, he carried her wet body out of the bathroom and into the bedroom. "You were beyond nasty, darling."

Her lips parted in surprise. "You didn't like it?"

Griffin smiled at Belinda as if she were a child. "I loved it." He placed her on the bed and lay beside her, unmindful of the water from their bodies soaking the sheets. He loved her and making love to her. Staring down into the eyes the color of dark coffee, he knew their relationship had changed with the wanton coupling. Belinda Eaton was sexy, passionate *and* incredibly nasty—the way he liked her.

Fatigue pressed Belinda down to the mattress like a lead blanket. It took Herculean strength to keep her eyes open. She fought valiantly but Morpheus proved victorious. "Good night, darling."

"Good night, baby."

Griffin, supporting his head on folded arms, stared up at the ceiling. He lay motionless, startled by the sudden thought that flashed through his mind. How had he forgotten about the man in Florida who'd claimed Belinda first?

And he wasn't so vain or naive to believe that just because Belinda opened her legs to him it meant she would open her heart to him. After all, he'd slept with women he liked, but didn't and would never love.

He was in too deep and didn't know how to extricate himself.

Never had he missed his brother as he did now. Grant had been the levelheaded older brother, wise beyond his years, and whenever he went to Grant in a quandary he came away buoyed with confidence.

He closed his eyes when, without warning, a wave of sadness held him captive then fled as quickly as it'd come. *If she's worth it, then fight like hell for her,* said a voice in his head that sounded remarkably like Grant's.

"Thank you, brother," Griffin whispered. He had his answer.

Chapter 12

Belinda and Griffin waited in the schoolyard along with other seventh-grade parents for the bus transporting their children from Gettysburg, Pennsylvania.

She'd elected to wait in his sport-utility vehicle, reading, while Griffin was engaged in a lively conversation with several men. The topic invariably turned to sports: baseball, football and hockey.

What garnered Belinda's rapt attention was that several women had drifted over to join the small group of men. They seemed to linger on the periphery until one was bold enough to rest her hand on Griffin's shoulder.

What the... Belinda caught herself before she screamed out the open window that she could look, but not touch. She sat motionless, watching the woman become more and more brazen until Griffin reached over to remove her hand. Within minutes her hand was back, this time on his back.

Griffin felt the warmth of the hand pressed to his back, and he curbed the urge to grab her wrist and fling it off. He glared at the woman who'd insisted on crossing his personal boundaries to touch him without permission. Now he understood Belinda's insistence on it.

What annoyed him was that the others hadn't invited the petite doll-like woman with a profusion of neatly braided hair flowing down her back to join the conversation. Glancing at her left hand he noticed it was bare. He found her attractive, but whatever she was offering he didn't want or need. Cupping her elbow, he led her away from the small crowd that was speculating whether the Flyers would make the Stanley Cup finals.

Bending closer to her ear, he affected a tight smile. "See that woman sitting in the white hybrid staring at us?" The woman nodded. "She happens to be my wife. I told her to stay in the car because she didn't take her medication this morning, and whenever that happens she tends to be a little violent. So I suggest you go back and stand with your friends, because once she goes off I have a hard time trying to control her."

A pair of round eyes widened with his disclosure. "You mean she's violent?" He nodded slowly. "Thanks for the heads-up."

Instead of returning to the men he headed to his vehicle and got in beside Belinda. "Don't you dare say anything," he warned, deadpan.

Belinda averted her eyes to conceal the grin stealing

its way over her face. "I would've helped you out if you didn't look as if you were enjoying her so much."

Griffin crossed his arms over his chest. "You did help me out."

Shifting, she noted his smug expression. "What?" Belinda's jaw dropped when she listened to Griffin's explanation for thwarting his admirer. "Medication, Griffin? You told her I was crazy?"

"Aw, baby, don't take it that way. I had to tell her something or she would've come home with us."

"I don't think so, love," Belinda drawled. "She would've gone home with *you,* not us."

"Four women in my life are enough, thank you."

A slight frown furrowed her brow. "Who's the fourth?"

"Gloria Rice."

Belinda nodded. How could she have forgotten her nieces' other grandmother? There came a flurry of activity as parents and their children spilled out of vehicles as the tour bus maneuvered into the schoolyard.

Griffin placed his hand on Belinda's arm. "Wait here. I'll get their luggage."

"What's the matter? You don't want anyone to see the crazy woman?"

He rolled his eyes at her. "Are you ever going to let me live this down?"

"I'll think about it," she teased.

A smile softened her features when she saw Sabrina, followed by Layla step off the bus. They appeared exhausted. Any semblance of a hairstyle was missing from both girls. Sabrina had parted her hair in the middle, but it appeared as if she couldn't decide whether to braid it or leave it loose. Layla had half a dozen braids, secured with colorful bands, shielding her face, while a thick plait hung down her back. They had two days to recover from their weeklong educational trip before returning to classes. It would become their last extended break until the end of the school term.

Shifting on her seat, Belinda smiled at her nieces when they slipped onto the second row of seats. "Welcome home."

"Hi, Aunt Lindy," they mumbled in unison.

"Are you girls hungry?"

Layla closed her eyes. "No, Aunty Lindy. I just want to take a bath and go to bed."

"Me, too," Sabrina said around the yawn she concealed behind her hand.

"We're not going to stop to eat," Belinda informed Griffin when he slipped behind the wheel. "They're exhausted."

Griffin nodded. "Home it is."

It took a full day before Sabrina and Layla reverted to their chatty selves. They climbed into bed with Belinda and talked nonstop about the buildings they'd visited in Washington, D.C., the historic preserved city of Williamsburg, Virginia, and Gettysburg National Military Park and Gettysburg National Cemetery.

They listened intently when Belinda related the events of the Battle of Gettysburg. "The battle began on July first and didn't end until the third of July, eighteen sixty-three. Not only was it one of the bloodiest battles of the Civil War, but it was significant because it marked the northernmost point reached by the Confederate army. It also marked the end of rebel supremacy on the battlefield."

Layla shifted into a more comfortable position as

she rested her head on a mound of pillows. "Why was that, Aunt Lindy?"

Belinda smiled at her nieces flanking her. "Confederate General Robert E. Lee had crossed the Mason-Dixon line into Pennsylvania for strategic and logistical reasons. The general was a student of another famous general, Napoleon Bonaparte, who had the audacity to use small forces against larger ones. Now historians differ as to why General Lee ventured into Northern territory. Some say he was foraging for shoes for his troops, while others claim Lee was overconfident because he'd defeated Union General Joseph Hooker at Chancellorsville."

"Where's Chancellorsville?" Sabrina asked.

"Virginia," Belinda said, smiling. Her nieces, who admitted to not liking history, had taken a sudden interest in it as the result of their class trip. "Whatever his reason it spelled ultimate defeat for the rebel forces."

"Why did the battle last so long?" Sabrina questioned.

"I have a book on Civil War battles you can read."

Layla made a face. "Aunt Lindy, we don't have time to read other books. Please tell us."

Just like they'd done when the girls were much younger and slept over at Belinda's house, she'd gather them in her bed and tell them stories about the lives of enslaved Africans and free men, the Underground Railroad, the Great Depression and the wars spanning the Revolutionary to Vietnam rather than the ubiquitous fairy tales. It had taken a week for the historical fairy tales to become a reality when they'd come face-to-face with the history of their country.

She told of President Lincoln's criticism of General Meade who'd chosen not to pursue the defeated Confederates, as he had thought that immediate action would have shortened the war; although the conflict continued for another two years, the Union forces victory at Gettysburg proved to be the turning point in the war, while amassing the most devastating roster of casualties: fifty-one thousand, North and South combined.

When Belinda's voice faded and she waited for more questions that never came, she realized her nieces had fallen asleep. In the past she would carry each to their beds, but at twelve the girls were two inches shorter than her five-six height and weighed more than one hundred pounds. If Griffin had stayed she would've asked him to take them to their bedrooms.

Reaching over Layla, she turned off the lamp and then settled down to join her nieces as they slept soundly. Belinda forced herself not to dwell on sharing a bed with Griffin because whenever she recalled what they'd done to each other her body betrayed her.

A few times she'd asked herself if she'd fallen in love with Griffin after they slept together or if she had had feelings for him before. And the answer was always the same: she'd fallen in love with Griffin Rice when she was still a teenager, that she resented the women in the photographs who clung possessively to his arm because she'd wanted to be them. She'd regarded him as a skirt-chaser because it made him more unappealing.

How could she have been so wrong about a man their nieces adored? Cecil and Nigel, who had been over-joyed when they saw Sabrina and Layla, no longer growled or showed Griffin their tiny teeth. When he had sat on the floor they jumped all over him as he pretended to fight off their attack. The girls had joined the fracas and pandemonium had ensued with barking, screams from the girls and hysterical laughter from Griffin. Strange feelings always arose when she watched him interact with the puppies and his nieces. But it had been in that instant that Belinda knew he would make an incredible father.

Belinda started up her Volvo and backed it out of the driveway, always mindful of the schoolchildren making their way to bus stops. Sabrina and Layla had walked two blocks to a classmate's house to wait with her and her younger sister for the bus that stopped on their corner.

Since her nieces had come to live with her, Belinda had begun speaking to many of the mothers who lived in the neighborhood. Some had invited her to come to their homes for coffee, and her nearest neighbor had invited her and Griffin to a dinner party. And, with the warmer weather, cooking outdoors had become the norm.

Her cell phone rang and she smiled. She knew from the distinctive ring that Griffin was calling her. "Good morning, darling," she crooned, activating the Bluetooth device.

"Good morning, baby. How are you?"

Her smile faded. "I'll let you know at the end of classes." It would be her first day back since the high school shut down two days early for spring break.

There came a pause. "You don't have to play superwoman, Lindy."

"I would've rather you said Wonder Woman. Her outfit was sexier than Superwoman's."

"I'm not joking, Belinda."

A frown furrowed her forehead. "Neither am I, Griffin. I've had more than a week to deal with what happened, and I'm good."

"I don't want to have to tell you I told you so when you have a meltdown."

"What are you so worried about, Griffin? Are you afraid that if I lose it, you'll have to raise the girls by—"

"Don't say it," Griffin warned in a dangerously soft voice. "Please don't say what I think you're going to say. This is not about the girls. This is about you, Belinda."

"I'm not a fragile hothouse flower that will wilt if you touch me. I can take care of myself. Didn't I prove that when I fought off a rapist?"

"Physical scars are not the same as emotional scars."

Belinda blew out a breath. She knew no amount of arguing would get Griffin to believe that she wasn't going to suffer lasting effects from one of her students firing a gun in her classroom.

"I thought we talked about this, Griffin, and decided it was nothing."

"You decided it was nothing, Lindy, not me. If you exhibit any behavior that proves injurious to our children's emotional well-being I'm going to have to take action. They've been through enough without…"

Touching a button, she disconnected the call. She would not put up with any man threatening her. The threat had begun and ended with Joel Thurman. Her cell phone rang again and she turned it off. She didn't want to talk or argue with Griffin, not when she wanted to use the time to fortify herself for when she met with her students again.

Belinda arrived at the high school and parked in the area designated as faculty parking. She nodded to the science teacher she'd dated, quickening her pace to avoid talking to him. Reaching into her handbag she removed her photo ID and hung it around her neck. What she found strange was the absence of noise. Students stood around in small groups, talking quietly among themselves, while teachers and staff members filed silently into the school building.

The incident had brought home the reality that, in a moment of madness, someone with a gun could've possibly taken the life of a classmate, relative, teacher or staff.

As she clocked in, Belinda was aware of the surreptitious glances directed her way. Valerie Ritchie walked in and punched her card. "Come with me," Belinda whispered as she turned on her heels and left the office.

"How are you doing?" Valerie asked when they found an empty first-floor classroom.

"I'm okay, Valerie. I am really all right," she said when Valerie gave her a look of disbelief. "What do I have to do to convince everyone that I don't need tranquilizers, or that I'm not a candidate for a straitjacket."

Valerie leaned closer. "Weren't you scared?"

Belinda stared at the teacher who was never seen with a hair out of place or her makeup less than perfect. Valerie had given an award-winning performance as a politician's wife, and although she was no longer in that role she continued to play the part.

"Of course I was frightened. But once I realized Sean Greer posed more of a threat to himself than to me or the other students in my class I stopped being afraid. You had to be there to hear him talking to the negotiator. He was nothing more than a frightened kid who just wanted to fit in—be accepted. Unfortunately, Brent Wiley got to him first."

What Belinda didn't reveal to Valerie was that she'd

been afraid that Sean was thinking of shooting himself when he'd placed the gun to his head. And, when she'd asked Griffin about helping to get competent legal counsel for the troubled youth, he'd told her that his friend had agreed to defend him pro bono.

The bell rang, signaling the beginning of classes, followed by an announcement from the principal that assemblies for each grade would be held throughout the day with counselors available to answer questions or talk one-on-one to students who requested individual sessions.

Belinda and Valerie exchanged a familiar look. The fallout from the school shooting would claim another day.

Belinda returned home to find Griffin's SUV parked in her driveway. He was seated on the chaise in her sitting room, waiting for her, his impassive expression revealing nothing.

She flashed a warm smile. "Good afternoon."

"Is it?"

"Of course it is, Griffin. I survived my first day back." Spinning around on her toes, she extended her arms. "See, no bullet holes." She wasn't given a chance to get her balance when she found herself pulled against Griffin's chest.

"Don't play with me, Belinda, or I'll—"

"Or you'll what!" she screamed at him. "Or you'll take my children from me? Is that what you were going to say? I don't think so, Griffin Rice. I don't care what kind of legal connections you think you have, but if you…"

An explosive kiss stopped her outburst. Belinda fought Griffin, but she was no match for his superior strength as his sensual assault shattered her fragile defenses. She found herself swimming through a haze of feelings she didn't want to feel and a desire so strong that it frightened her with its intensity.

His fingers eased around her wrists as he pulled her arms behind her back, holding her captive. "Don't ever hang up on me again," he warned softly.

Belinda stared up at him through her lashes. "I wouldn't have had to hang up on you if you hadn't threatened me."

Lifting her effortlessly with one arm, Griffin made his way out of the sitting room to her bed. "I didn't threaten you, Lindy."

"Yes, you did," she managed to say as her back made contact with the mattress. "I…" For the second time within minutes she found herself speechless.

Griffin's hands were busy searching under her skirt for the waistband of her panty hose. In one smooth motion, her hose and panties lay on the floor and her legs were anchored over his shoulders.

"No, Griffin! Please!"

Pleas became sobs of ecstasy as Griffin utilized his own method to defuse her anger, and the degree to which she responded to his raw, sensuous lovemaking left her shaking uncontrollably. She surrendered completely to his rapacious tongue, drowning in the passion that left her shaking and crying at the same time.

Griffin lowered her legs and moved up her body. He kissed her deeply, permitting Belinda to taste herself on his tongue. "Now, can we talk?"

Belinda pushed against his shoulder. She didn't want to talk. All she wanted to do was sleep. "Not now, Griffin."

He smiled. "When, baby?"

"Later."

Griffin's smile grew wider. Making love to Belinda

was the perfect antidote for defusing her temper. She was snoring lightly when he undressed her and pulled a nightgown over her head. He retreated to the half bath, soaped a washcloth and returned to the bedroom to clean away the evidence of their lovemaking. He'd covered her with a sheet and blanket when he heard the distinctive chime indicating someone had opened a door.

He met Sabrina and Layla as they dropped their backpacks and headed toward the rear of the house to see their pets. "What do you want for dinner?"

Layla stopped, giving him a bright smile. "Aunt Lindy said she was going to make spaghetti and meatballs."

Griffin didn't tell his niece that if her aunt didn't get up in time to prepare dinner, he would. He had to make several business calls to the West Coast, but it was something he could accomplish either at his house or Belinda's.

He planned to stay the night despite the fact it wasn't the weekend. Spending eight consecutive days with Belinda had spoiled him. Not only had he fallen in love with her but missed her whenever they were apart.

How had it happened so quickly? How had he fallen so hard for a woman he'd known for years? The questions continued to plague him later that night as he lay on the sofa bed waiting for sleep to overtake him, when he didn't have to think of the woman who made him plan for a future that included her as his wife and the mother of their children.

Chapter 13

Griffin's hands drummed rhythmically on the steering wheel when he stopped for a red light, mimicking the hand clapping in "Hand Jive," the infectious song from the classic musical *Grease*.

He'd come to know most of the words from the play over the past month because Layla and Sabrina had decided to participate in their school's musical production for the first time. Layla had auditioned for a singing part in the production, while Sabrina worked behind the scenes, using her budding artistic skill on set decorations.

They stayed after classes to rehearse and as the day for the actual performance neared they'd begun full-day weekend rehearsals.

Belinda had scoured Philadelphia's thrift and vintage shops for replicas of poodle skirts and saddle shoes. In the end she had to resort to the Internet to gather the

names of collectors of 1950s memorabilia. Her perse-
verance paid off, because she'd purchased an authentic
poodle skirt and a pair of black-and-white saddle shoes
that were a perfect fit for Layla.

He'd made arrangements with his mother for her
granddaughters to spend the night with her. Gloria and
Lucas had returned from their month-long vacation
cruise tanned, relaxed and looking forward to spending
time with their granddaughters.

Layla leaned forward in her seat and tapped Griffin's
shoulder. "Uncle Griff, please repeat that track."

Griffin pressed a button on the dashboard, tapped his
finger on the steering wheel while the interior of the car
was filled with the catchy tune. Layla and Sabrina
shared a smile when their uncle's voice joined theirs.
They'd always liked their Uncle Griff, but since he'd
become their stepfather they'd come to love him as if
he were their father.

They went to him to enlist his aid when they wanted
something they knew their aunt would probably not
approve of. His "I'll discuss it with her" usually pre-
dicted success, if not a compromise which they were
always ready to accept.

Griffin took a right turn down the street that led to
Gloria Rice's condo. "Make certain you finish your
homework before your aunt and I pick you up tomorrow night."

"We will," the two girls chorused.

He and Belinda were scheduled to attend a political
fund-raiser later that evening and Saturday evening
Sabrina and Layla were invited to birthday sleep-over
for a classmate who lived nearby.

Maneuvering into a space set aside for visitor

parking, Griffin shut off the engine. The girls gathered their overnight bags and together they made their way to the modern doorman building. He gave his name to the uniformed man who rang Gloria's apartment to let her know that she had visitors.

"She's expecting you, Mr. Rice. The elevator to her apartment is on the right."

Sabrina, waiting until the elevator doors closed behind them said, "Why does he have to say *'she's expecting you, Mr. Rice'* when he already knows you're Grandma's son?"

Griffin gave his niece a direct stare. "That's what's known as doing one's job. He has rules or a protocol to follow, and no matter who comes into the building he has to follow the rule that all visitors must be announced."

"It sounds like a silly rule to me," Layla mumbled under her breath.

"Would it be so silly if he let someone into the building whose intent is to rob or hurt a tenant?" Griffin asked.

"No, Uncle Griff, that's different," Layla argued.

"No, it isn't, Layla. What if someone who looks exactly like me decides he wants to burglarize Grandma's apartment and the doorman just let him walk in. Legally the owner of the building would be responsible for the loss because the doormen are his employees."

The elevator came to a stop, and the doors opened smoothly. Griffin stepped out, holding the door while his nieces filed out and made their way down the carpeted hallway to where Gloria stood outside the door waiting for them. Cradling their faces between her hands, she kissed each girl on the cheek. Griffin wanted to tell his mother that her granddaughters had reached the age where they shied away from public displays of affection, but decided to hold his tongue.

Leaning over, he kissed his mother. "Hey, beautiful."

Gloria swatted at his shoulder. "Save that stuff for someone who isn't as gullible as your mother."

Griffin smiled at her. "When have you known me to lie?"

Gloria angled her head, seemingly deep in thought. "Not too often." Her expression brightened. "Can you spare a few minutes to share a cup of coffee with your mother, or do you have to run?"

"I have some time."

"Come sit in the kitchen while I brew a cup."

Slipping off his jacket, Griffin hung it on the coat tree near the door. He'd come with Gloria when she talked about purchasing a unit either in a renovated or new building going up in the gentrified Spring Garden neighborhood. He'd wanted her to purchase the one-bedroom unit, but Gloria had insisted that she needed the additional bedroom for whenever her granddaughters came for a visit. Layla and Sabrina loved visiting because it was closer to downtown Philadelphia with its theaters, museums, restaurants, department stores and specialty shops.

Gloria Rice had downsized her life and the furnishings in her apartment reflected her new lifestyle. Every piece of furniture had a purpose and the pale monochromatic color scheme reflected simplicity at its best.

Griffin followed his mother into an immaculate ultramodern stainless-steel kitchen. "What are you cooking for dinner?"

"I'm not," Gloria said as she reached for a coffee pod from a rack on the countertop. "I asked the girls what they wanted me to cook and they said they wanted to eat out."

"Have you decided where?"

Gloria's eyes sparkled when she smiled. "I told them it can be their choice."

"You're spoiling them, Mom."

"And you don't, son? I'm their grandmother and that gives me the right to spoil them rotten. You, on the other hand, don't have the same rights."

Griffin stared at his mother dressed in a stylish linen pantsuit. The reddish-orange color flattered the former librarian's dark complexion. "As a dad I do."

Reaching for a cup in an overhead cabinet, Gloria placed it under the coffee-brewing machine then pushed a button to start the process. "You enjoy being a father." The question was a statement.

Bending his tall body to fit into the chair in the dining nook, Griffin nodded. "I do. At first I kept telling myself that I couldn't do it, that I'd fail miserably, but thanks to Belinda I've been holding my own."

Resting a hip against a granite-topped countertop, Gloria met her son's direct stare. "I never thought I'd say this, but I'm going to anyway. Belinda's a better mother than her sister. Donna was totally disorganized and much too lax with her daughters. When I told her that the girls left their clothes wherever they stepped out of them her excuse was that was what she was there for—to pick up after them."

"Belinda changed that, Mom."

"I know. Layla called me when she got her cell phone to tell me about her new bedroom and study area. She also said she had to keep her room clean otherwise she and Sabrina would lose certain privileges."

Griffin nodded. "At first I thought Belinda was being a little too strict, but unlike Donna she's not a stay-at-home mother. She has enough to deal with at the high

school without having to come home and pick up after
teenagers."

There was only the sound of brewing coffee as
mother and son regarded each other. "She's good for the
girls and she's good for you," Gloria said after a comfortable pause.

"Belinda's an incredible mother, and an even more
incredible woman."

"I take it you like her." Griffin closed his eyes and
when he opened them they were filled with an emotion
Gloria had never seen before. There was no doubt her
son was taken with his nieces' godmother.

"It goes beyond liking, Mom. I'm in love with Belinda."

"Does she know it?"

Griffin shook his head. "I don't think so."

"When are you going to tell her?"

"I don't know. I suppose I'm waiting for the right time."

"There's never a right time when it comes to affairs
of the heart, Griffin Rice. You wait too long and you're
going to lose her."

"I'm not going to lose her."

"Why? Because you say so?"

A muscle quivered at Griffin's jaw. "No. Because it's
not going to happen."

Gloria saw movement out of the corner of her eye.
"What is it, Sabrina?"

"Layla wants chicken and waffles and I want a
hamburger."

"Don't worry, sweets. We'll find a restaurant where
Layla can get her chicken and waffles and you your
burger."

"Thank you, Grandma."

"You're welcome, Sabrina. I can't believe they're

growing up so quickly," Gloria remarked after Sabrina returned to the spare bedroom she shared with her sister whenever they came to visit.

"That's what frightens me, Mom. What am I going to do when the boys come knocking on the door?"

"You'll know what to do when the time comes."

"I hope you're right."

"Do you think it'd be any easier if they were boys?" Gloria asked.

"Yeah, I think so. At least I'd be able to tell them what *not* to do."

Gloria added a teaspoon of sugar and a splash of cream to the cup when the brewing cycle ended, handing it to her son. "Stop stressing yourself, Griffin. Everything will work out okay."

Gloria's "everything will work out okay" played over and over in Griffin's head during his return drive to Belinda's house. And, when he opened the door to find her standing in the middle of her bedroom in her underwear, he told himself that his mother was right. As long as he had Belinda in his life he didn't have anything to worry about.

Crossing the room, he brushed a kiss over her mouth. "I'll be ready as soon as I shave and shower."

Belinda walked into the grand ballroom of the Ritz-Carlton, her hand tucked in the bend of Griffin's elbow over the sleeve of his tuxedo jacket. The night was warm enough for her to drape just a silk shawl over the customary little black dress. The one-shoulder satin-organza with a generous front slit showed off her legs and matching Christian Louboutin four-inch pumps with each step. Her stylist had cut her hair, and it highlighted the roundness of her face when it feathered around her delicate jawline.

She'd taken special care with her makeup, applying smoky and raspberry colors to her lids, cheeks and lips. It had been a while since her last black-tie affair, and it was fun to dress up for the event.

Griffin was breathtakingly, drop-dead gorgeous, and as comfortable in formal attire as he was in casual clothes. He'd elected to wear a platinum-tone silk tie with his tuxedo rather than the usual black.

The event was to raise funds for an up-and-coming politician who'd announced his intent to challenge the controversial, but very popular incumbent mayor. It wasn't until Belinda was introduced to the charismatic mayoral candidate that she learned that he and Griffin had attended law school together. Griffin had graduated first and the candidate number two in their class.

Patrick Garson's dark blue eyes took in everything about the woman beside Griffin Rice in one sweeping glance. Reaching for her hands, he brought one hand to his mouth and kissed her fingers. "Lovely. You are simply lovely—"

"Belinda," Griffin supplied. "Her name is Belinda Eaton. Belinda, this is my good friend and hopefully the next mayor of Philadelphia, Patrick Garson."

Belinda smiled and mouthed the appropriate responses. There was something about Patrick Garson that was too perfect. Not a strand was out of place in his wavy honey-blond hair. Even his sandy-brown eyebrows were perfect, and Belinda wondered whether he had them plucked or waxed. She approved of metrosexual men, but she believed men like Patrick were apt to spend a little too much time in the mirror.

"Pat, darling. Oh, there you are," a woman drawled with a thick Southern inflection.

Belinda turned to find a statuesque blonde heading in their direction. The light from the chandeliers overhead glinted off the large solitaire on her left hand. Smiling, she looped her arm through Patrick's.

Barbie and Ken. A knowing smile touched Belinda's lips. Patrick and the woman who probably was his fiancée were the perfect prototypes for the popular dolls.

Her topaz-blue eyes lit up when she spied Griffin. "Griff, darling. How are you?"

Griffin touched his cheek to hers. "I'm good, Jessica. How are you?"

Holding out her arms, Jessica spun around on her designer stilettos. "As you can see, I'm really good. It was a bitch trying to lose the last ten pounds, but I did it."

Belinda stared at Jessica, stunned. The woman was practically skin and bones. She was at least five-eleven in her bare feet, and probably weighed less than Belinda.

Wrapping an arm around Belinda's waist, Griffin pulled her against his length. "Belinda, I'd like to introduce you to another of my law school friends. This is Jessica Ricci, Pat's fiancée and hopefully the next first lady of Philadelphia. Jessica, Belinda Eaton."

Jessica flashed her practiced smile, exhibiting a mouth of perfect porcelain veneers. "I'm charmed to meet you, Belinda. Please call me Jessie. Jessica sounds so staid."

Belinda couldn't help but return the friendly infectious smile that crinkled the blonde's brilliant eyes. "Then Jessie it is."

"Are you a lawyer, too?" she drawled.

"No. I'm a teacher."

"Do you teach the little babies?"

Shaking her head and smiling, Belinda said, "No. I teach at the high school level."

"How do you keep the boys from coming on to you?"

Belinda felt the heat from Griffin's gaze when he stared at her. It was the same question he'd put to her, what seemed so long ago. "I don't entertain their advances."

Griffin's fingers tightened. "Belinda and I are going to get something from the bar, then we're going to circulate. I'll call you later, Pat, and we'll set up something where the four of us can get together without reporters and photographers shadowing you."

Patrick patted Griffin's shoulder. "I'll be waiting for your call."

"Thanks," Belinda whispered under her breath as Griffin led her across the ballroom to one of three bars set up around the perimeter.

"I should've warned you about Jessica. She's a little chatty, but she's perfect for Patrick."

"They remind me of Ken and Barbie dolls."

Griffin chuckled. "One time we had a Halloween party and they came dressed as Ken and Barbie."

"Does she have an eating disorder?"

"No. She had an accident several years back, and a doctor put her on cortisone, which made her put on about fifty pounds. She finally came off the medication and it took two years of diet and exercise to lose the weight."

"Are you supporting him because he's a friend, or because you feel he's the best candidate for the office?"

"Both," Griffin stated emphatically. "Patrick has one of the most brilliant minds of anyone I've met or known. He would make a very good mayor." His gaze lingered on Belinda's mouth. Patrick had called her lovely—and that she was. "Now, what can I get you to drink?"

"I'll have a white wine."

His eyebrows lifted. "Are you sure you don't want anything stronger?"

"Very sure, darling. I've appointed myself the designated driver for tonight, so I don't want to overdo it."

Griffin leaned closer. "I'm going to have to have one drink, so you don't have to worry about my being impaired."

"I'll still have the white…" Her words trailed off when she spied someone she hadn't seen in years. "Excuse me, Griffin. I'll be right back."

He stood motionless, watching Belinda as she wove her way through the throng crowding in the ballroom. He wasn't aware that he'd been holding his breath until he saw her talking to a woman who looked vaguely familiar.

Belinda tapped the shoulder of a woman with skin the color of palomino-gold. Surprise, then shock froze the features of Zabrina Cooper when she turned around.

"Belinda."

"Zabrina Mixon." There was no emotion in Belinda's voice.

"It's Cooper. I've gone back to using my maiden name."

Belinda stared at the incredibly beautiful woman who, if she'd married Myles, would've become her sister-in-law. But weeks before they were scheduled to exchange vows, Zabrina ended the engagement and married a much older man—a prominent Pennsylvania politician. And when she gave birth to a son nine months later, rumors were rampant that she'd been sleeping with Thomas Cooper while engaged to Myles Eaton.

Belinda wanted to hate the woman who'd embarrassed her family and broken her brother's heart. She'd felt personally responsible for the breakup, because she'd been the one to introduce her then-best friend to her brother.

"I'm sorry to hear about your husband."

"Don't feel sorry for me, Belinda. It's Adam who needs your sympathy. It's not easy for a ten-year-old to adjust to losing his father."

Belinda went completely still. It was apparent Zabrina wasn't going to play the grieving widow. "You never loved him, did you?"

"If you want to know the truth, Belinda, then I'm going to tell you the truth. I hated Thomas Cooper as much as I loved your brother."

Belinda recalled the images of Zabrina Cooper staring blankly at photographers when they snapped frames of her stoic face at her husband's funeral. Thomas Cooper had come from a long line of African American politicians dating back to the 1890s, and when the confirmed bachelor announced his engagement a collective groan went up from women all over the state. And nine months later when his young wife delivered a son, rumors as to his hasty nuptials were put to rest.

"If you hated him, then why did you marry him, Brina?"

Zabrina blinked back tears. It'd been years since anyone had called her Brina, and hearing it come from her childhood friend took her back to a time when all was right and pure in her world.

"I can't tell you. I swore an oath that I'd never tell anyone."

Belinda moved closer. "You don't have to tell me if you don't want to."

"I need a friend, Belinda. When I married Thomas he made me get rid of all my friends."

Belinda felt her pain. "Do you have a piece of paper?"

"Why?"

"I want to give you my phone numbers. Maybe we can get together to have lunch or even dinner."

Opening her small evening bag, Zabrina took out her cell phone. "I'll program your numbers into my phone."

Three minutes later, the two women parted with a promise to get together to talk. They couldn't change the past, but Belinda knew Zabrina needed a friend.

"Wasn't that Thomas Cooper's widow?" Griffin asked when Belinda returned.

"Yes."

He'd heard rumors why Zabrina Mixon married a man old enough to be her father, but they'd remained just that—rumors. What he did know was that when she ended her engagement to Myles to marry Cooper she'd been vilified in the press until Thomas Cooper used his political influence to pull the articles.

Belinda accepted the glass of wine Griffin had ordered for her. "We're going to have lunch or dinner one of these days," she said after taking a sip of the cool liquid.

"Good for you."

"Oh, you approve?"

Griffin nodded. "Yes. Look at us, once we were able to clear the air about how we feel about each other."

"You're right, darling."

Griffin knew she liked him, but what he didn't know was how much she'd come to love him—enough to want to spend the rest of her life with him.

Chapter 14

Sabrina leaned closer to her sister as they sat in front of the computer monitor. "I don't like that dress."

Layla rolled her eyes. "You don't have to like it. We're just looking at different styles."

"Isn't it too soon to think of bridesmaid's dresses when Uncle Griff hasn't given her a ring?"

Layla's hand stilled on the mouse. "Wasn't it you who said you overheard him tell Grandma that he was in love with Aunt Lindy?"

"Yes, but that still doesn't mean they're going to get married."

"I just want to be ready in case they are ready. I know we'll be in the wedding, but I am not going to wear a dress I don't like."

Sabrina stared at her twin. "Maybe it's better if we

design the invitations first. Then the only thing we'll have to do is fill in the date."

"Okay," Layla conceded. "We'll do the invitations. What if we get some bridal magazines and look through them. It would be easier than trying to come up with our own designs."

"That's a good idea. Let's ask Uncle Griff if he can take us to the mall."

Layla shook her head. "I don't know if he's going to take us again. We were just there yesterday."

Sabrina pursed her mouth. "I could always tell him that we need to get a gift for Aunt Lindy's birthday."

"Let's do it," Layla said, shutting down the computer.

Belinda's cell phone rang, and she reached over to the table next to her rocker to retrieve it. She pushed the talk button without glancing at the display. "Hello."

"Hello, Belinda."

She sat up after recognizing the voice coming through the earpiece. "Raymond. Long time, no hear. Where are you?"

"I'm still in Orlando, but I'm coming up your way next week. Do you think you can find some time to see me?"

"Where are you going to be?"

"I have to attend a conference at Johns Hopkins, but I can stop in Philly for a few days either before or after."

"You're going to have to give me a date, Raymond. My nieces are living with me now, and I have very little free time."

"How do you like playing mother?"

A slight frown appeared between her eyes. "I'm not 'playing mother,' Raymond. I am a mother."

"I'm sorry about that."

She smiled. "Apology accepted. Look, Raymond, I'm not in the house right now so there's no way for me to check my planner. Can you call me tomorrow evening and I'll let you know when we can get together?"

"You've got it, doll. Good afternoon."

"Good afternoon, Raymond."

Belinda looked at Griffin staring back at her. He'd overheard her conversation with Raymond. "Raymond's coming up next week."

"I thought paroled cons weren't allowed to leave the state," Griffin said, deadpan.

"That's enough, Griffin."

Griffin left the cushioned love seat on Belinda's front porch and came over to hunker down in front of her. "Sunshine's coming up next week and what, Belinda? Are you going to ask me to take care of the girls while you open your legs for him?"

"Stop it!" Her eyes filled with tears. "You have so little respect for me that you think I'd sleep with two men at the same time?"

"What's with you and this dude?"

"He's a friend, Griffin. A friend I'm not sleeping with," she added in a softer tone.

"Of course you're not sleeping with him because you're sleeping with me. But what's going to happen when he comes up?"

Suddenly it dawned on Belinda that Griffin was jealous—jealous of a man he'd never met. "Nothing's going to happen. I told him that I have the girls living with me, so he's going to stay at a hotel."

"And what if the girls weren't living with you. Where would he stay?"

"In my guest bedroom."

Griffin blinked once. "You really mean that you're just *friends?*"

She threw up a hand. "Yes, Griffin Rice! We are *f-r-i-e-n-d-s!*" She spelled the word for him.

A smile lit up Griffin's face like the rising sun. "Well, damn, Eaton. Why didn't you say that in the first place?"

"I did, Rice," she countered. "You just chose to believe what you wanted to believe, that a woman can't be friends with a man and not sleep with him."

"I've had women as friends that I didn't sleep with."

Belinda emitted an unladylike snort. "Yeah, right."

He leaned closer. "We were friends before we started sleeping together."

She ran a finger down the length of his nose. "Wrong, Rice. We were in-laws before we started sleeping together."

"We're still in-laws."

"True," Belinda drawled.

Reaching for her wrist, Griffin eased Belinda off the rocker and onto the floor of the porch. "I've been doing some thinking about hanging out here during the week and at my place on the weekends."

"You know you're dangerous when you start thinking," she said teasingly.

"I'm serious, Belinda."

She sobered. "Talk to me."

His eyes were fathomless pools of dark brown when he focused on Belinda's mouth. "Why don't we blend households?"

"Please explain blending, because I thought that's what we've done."

"Either you live with me, or I'll live with you."

Belinda shook her head. "Isn't that what we're doing, Griffin? You spend more time here during the week than you do in Paoli. And there're very few weekends we're not in Paoli. So, I don't know what it is you want."

Griffin took a deep breath. "I want you, me and the girls to live together under one roof."

For a moment, Belinda let herself believe she was mistaken when she tried analyzing the complex man sitting beside her. "You want us to shack up together?"

"Live together."

"Live. Shack. Same difference."

"What do you think?"

"I think you're crazy. What message would we send to our nieces if we shack up together?"

"It doesn't have to be 'shacking up,' as you put it."

"Pray tell, Rice, what would it be?"

"We could get married."

Belinda stared at Griffin Rice as if he'd taken leave of his senses. He'd mentioned marriage as if he were negotiating a deal. *Give me this and I'll concede that.* And, she wondered, what provoked his spur-of-the-moment proposal?

The sex was great—no, it was better than great. It was incredible. And what about love? Did he actually believe she would marry him when not once had he said or indicated that he loved her?

A hint of a smile ghosted across her face as realization dawned, just as the sky cleared with the sun rising each morning. "This is about Raymond, isn't it?"

"Who?" Griffin asked, feigning ignorance.

"Sunshine. This is about him, isn't it? You still don't believe that we have a platonic relationship and if I became your wife then you'd make certain he'd be out of my life—permanently. Thanks, but no thanks, Griffin. I don't want to marry you."

"This is not about Sunshine."

"Who is it about, Griffin, because it's definitely not about *us*." Pushing to her feet, she stood up and went into the house, leaving him staring into space.

The soft slam of the door caught his attention and Griffin thought Belinda had come back because she'd changed her mind. He schooled his features so not to reveal his disappointment when Sabrina and Layla came out of the house.

Sabrina stared at her sister. "Uncle Griff, can you please drive us to the mall?"

He frowned. "Didn't we have this conversation yesterday?"

"Yes," Layla said quickly. "But we forgot to buy something for Aunt Lindy's birthday."

Griffin stood up. "When's her birthday?"

"May twenty-eighth," the girls said in unison.

He wanted to tell his nieces that he didn't want to go back to a mall two days in a row because he hated fighting the parking-lot traffic. He also detested the crowds. If they'd spent the weekend in Paoli then he would've driven them to a smaller mall that featured specialty shops instead of the large department stores.

Mother's Day had come and gone and the day hadn't gone well with the teenagers. They spent the day in their rooms, refusing to go to their grandparents' house for Sunday dinner.

It ended when he sat down with them to let both girls know how much Belinda had been hurt by their behavior, but that she understood they missed their mother, that although she would never replace their mother she loved them as if she'd given birth to them. The day ended with the four of them crawling into Belinda's bed and falling asleep.

He woke hours later and carried the girls to their bed, then drove back to Paoli. Griffin didn't know how Belinda did it. She made parenting look so easy when in reality it was the hardest job in the world.

Reaching into the pocket of his jeans, he took out his car keys.

"Let's go."

"We have to get our money," Layla said excitedly.

"I'll cover you this time," Griffin offered.

The two girls exchanged a glance. Sabrina smiled at her uncle. "We have to get our purses."

"Hurry up." His voice was fraught with resignation. He didn't know what it was with women and handbags. It was as if they couldn't go anywhere without a purse attached to their wrist or shoulder.

Griffin found himself sitting on a tufted chair in a jewelry shop while a saleswoman showed Sabrina and Layla gold lockets.

Layla beckoned to him. "Come, Uncle Griff, and look at this one. Do you think Aunt Lindy would like it?"

He stood and came over to the counter. His nieces had selected a variety of heart-shaped lockets. "Which ones do you like?" They pointed to two lockets. "I like this one," he said, pointing to one with a diamond on the front.

"We don't have enough money for that one," Sabrina said.

He pulled her ponytail. "Don't worry about the price. Pick out whatever you want."

Griffin wandered over to the showcase with diamond

engagement rings and wedding bands. He spied one that would look perfect on Belinda's hand. Motioning to a salesman, he pointed in the case. "I want to see that one."

Light from hanging lamps caught the brilliance of the diamond solitaire. He didn't know if it would fit Belinda, but he didn't care. "I'll take it," he said softly. "I don't want my daughters to know I'm buying this for their mother, so let's not make a big show of it." Reaching into his pocket, he took out a case with his credit cards. He pushed one across the counter, winking when the elderly man smiled at him.

"What did you buy, Uncle Griff?" Sabrina asked when she saw him with the small shopping bag.

"It's just a little something for your aunt's birthday. Are you finished shopping?" he asked, smoothly changing the topic.

"We're going downstairs to the bookstore while you pay for the necklace. We'll meet you in front of the store."

Not waiting for their uncle to agree or disagree, the two girls raced out of the jewelry store. They needed to buy some magazines to get an idea of what they wanted to wear to their aunt and uncle's wedding.

Belinda's palms tingled from applauding as the entire cast of the school production of *Grease* came back for a third curtain call. She was startled when Griffin put two fingers in his mouth and whistled loud enough to shatter her eardrums. The spring concert was a rousing success.

Belinda had found herself singing along with Sandy and the Pink Ladies, and she was surprised when Griffin knew the lyrics to "Greased Lightning."

Both sets of grandparents had come to see the production, but Dwight and Roberta declined Lucas and

Gloria's invitation to come with them to take their granddaughters out to an ice-cream parlor because they'd committed to a dinner-dance and they would already be late, but they hadn't wanted to miss seeing their grandchildren's dramatic debut.

Belinda kissed her mother and father, resplendent in evening attire, and watched as they rushed out of the auditorium. "Let's wait out in the lobby for the girls," she shouted to be overheard.

Slowly, they inched their way down the aisle and out of the auditorium to the lobby of the elite, private school. Sabrina and Layla would enter the ninth grade the next school year, and then she and Griffin would have to select a high school commensurate with their academic standards.

They'd attended a public school from the first to the third grade, accelerating to the fifth grade when they showed advanced aptitude. But at their present school, every student was gifted.

They didn't have to wait long as Sabrina and Layla appeared—both in stage makeup. Layla wore a cardigan sweater, buttoned in the back, poodle skirt, bobby socks and black-and-white saddle shoes. She'd tied a scarf around her neck and another around her ponytail.

Both girls squealed in excitement when Lucas and Gloria handed them bouquets of flowers. Lucas hunkered down and made a big show of kissing each girl on the cheek. "The flowers are from both your grandma and grandpa. They had to leave. What's in the shopping bags is something else Grandma and I brought back for you." They'd bought so many souvenirs for the girls they'd decided not to give them everything at the same time.

Layla smiled and leaned closer to Lucas. "Can we look now?"

"No, baby girl. Open it when you get home."

Sabrina squinted at Lucas. "Grandpa, we're much too old to be baby girls."

Lucas tugged on the end of her ponytail. "I don't care if you're thirty, you'll always be a baby girl to me."

Griffin patted his father's shoulder. "Dad, it's time we leave before we won't be able to get a seat."

Nodding, Lucas rose to his feet. "The girls can ride with me and Glo."

Griffin winked at his mother. "We'll meet you there."

"Your father has really mellowed," Belinda said as Griffin headed in the direction of the ice-cream parlor.

"Yeah. That's what Mom says. She claims going away together was the best thing for him."

"For him, or for them, Griffin?"

"I think it was good for both of them. They needed time away to deal with whatever they needed to deal with."

Chapter 15

Griffin sat in the shiny lipstick-red booth with his mother and Layla, while Sabrina, Belinda and Lucas sat opposite them. They'd ordered floats and sundaes smothered with endless toppings.

"This is decadent and fattening," Gloria said, spooning ice cream, whipped cream and chopped nuts into her mouth.

Layla picked colorful candies off her sundae. "My favorite is Gummi Bears."

Griffin smiled at his mother. "Didn't you join a gym?"

"I did, but the question should be, do I go."

Lucas stared at his ex-wife. "I'll go with you when I'm not working."

Sabrina patted her grandfather's arm. "Do you still work at the hospital, Grandpa?"

"No, sweetheart. I retired from the hospital pharmacy and now work part-time."

"Is that good?"

He nodded. "It's very good. I have a lot more time to do all the things I've always wanted to do."

Layla took a sip of water. "Grandpa, can you take Breena and me with you when you go to Europe again?"

"That depends on your aunt and uncle. We can't take you anywhere unless they say it's okay."

"Is it okay?" the girls asked in unison.

Belinda looked directly at Griffin. "We have to talk about it."

"And it all depends," Griffin added.

"On what?" they chorused.

"On your grades *and* how well you do your chores."

Layla rolled her eyes. "Now you sound like Aunt Lindy."

Griffin lowered his eyebrows. "You didn't know your Aunt Lindy and I are a team?"

Sabrina sucked her teeth. "I knew that. I heard you talking to Grandma and you told her that you love Aunt Lindy."

A silence descended on the table so thick it was palpable as the six people in the booth exchanged glances. "Did I say something I wasn't supposed to say?" Sabrina whispered, as if telling a secret.

Gloria glared across the table at her granddaughter. "You're not supposed to listen in on other people's conversations. And if you do, then you're not supposed to repeat it."

"I wasn't listening in, Grandma. I just happened to walk in the kitchen while he was talking to you. Besides, he was talking loud. If it was a secret, then he should've been whispering."

Belinda's heart beat rapidly against her ribs with Sabrina's revelation. Griffin had told his mother that he loved her and he hadn't told her.

The nerve of him! The absolute nerve of him!

Gloria touched a napkin to her mouth. "I don't know about anyone else, but I'm ready to turn in. Belinda, would you mind if the girls stayed with me tonight? After all, there's no school tomorrow."

"Yes, Mom, they can stay." Griffin had answered for Belinda. He knew she wanted answers, answers only he could give her. And, if she went off on him he didn't want the girls around to hear them arguing. He didn't want to subject them to what he and Grant had gone through as children.

"I asked, Belinda, Griffin," Gloria admonished softly.

"I'm sorry, Mom."

Belinda blinked as if shocked back to reality. "Yes, Mrs. Rice, they can stay over."

Gloria gave her a saccharine smile. "I think it's time you either call me Mom or Gloria. It's up to you."

Belinda returned her smile. "Thank you—Mom."

Sliding out of the booth, Griffin reached into his pocket and tossed a bill on the table. Extending his hand, he gently helped Gloria out of the booth. "We'll bring over a change of clothes when we come to pick them up tomorrow."

"Don't rush, son. I'll give them something to wear. It may not be their style, but it'll keep them clothed." Tiptoeing to reach him, Gloria kissed Griffin's cheek. "Good luck with Lindy."

"Thank you."

Griffin had thought he was alone when he'd told his mother that he was in love with Belinda and wanted to marry her. He was waiting for the end of the school year to tell her, but his niece had let the cat out of the bag. He had to deal with it now—not later.

Not a word passed between them during the drive from the ice-cream parlor to Griffin's house in Paoli. He had wanted to tell Belinda that he loved her—loved anything and everything about her. It wasn't just her passion, that she held nothing back when offering herself, but it was also her strength, intelligence, determination, dedication and devotion to her students and to their daughters. There was also the playfulness and wit, the way she shed her inhibitions when she was rolling on the floor with Cecil and Nigel. He loved her even when they didn't agree on child rearing, because they were totally committed to the twins' well-being.

Griffin closed his eyes rather than watch Belinda pace the length of the patio in Paoli. It wasn't that long ago that she'd ordered him to meet her on the porch at Donna and Grant's house so they could talk. That time it'd been about his buying gifts for their nieces, and now it was about *them*.

He opened his eyes at the same time a frown furrowed his smooth brow. "Lindy, please sit down and talk to me."

"Why, Griffin, did you have to tell your mother before you told me?"

"I planned to tell you, but I wanted to wait."

She stopped long enough to give him a hostile stare. "When? Eleven years from now?"

"No, darling. First, I wanted to wait until the school

year was over. I didn't want any distractions when we sat down to plan our future. Then, I changed my mind and wanted to tell you on your birthday."

"You can't plan a future with me if you don't tell me how you feel about me, Griffin Rice. You told your mother that you loved me. Don't you think it's time you tell me to my face?"

Griffin went to Belinda, pulling her gently into his embrace. "I love you, Belinda Jacqueline Eaton. I've loved you for a very long time, but you wouldn't let me get close to you. It took a tragedy—when I realized I'd lost my only sibling—to shake me to the core. But I will fight like hell to hold on to the only woman I've ever loved."

Belinda couldn't stop the tears that were welling up in her eyes from flowing. Her lower lip trembled. "I should kick your behind, Griffin Rice, for waiting all these years to tell me this. What happened to the bigshot, hard-nosed lawyer who will go to the mat for his clients, but can't tell a woman that he likes her?"

Cradling her face in his palms, Griffin wiped away her tears with his thumbs.

"I don't *like* you, Belinda. You like *me*. I *love* you!"

"No, Griffin. I don't like you."

"What!"

A trembling smile found its way over her face. "I love you, Griffin Rice. I love you," she repeated it over and over as he picked her up and swung her around.

Griffin stopped, lowering her feet to the patio floor. "I'm going to ask you to do something for me, not tonight, but soon."

Easing back, Belinda stared up into the eyes of the man she'd loved for so long that she couldn't remember when she didn't love him. "What is it?"

"Call Sunshine, and tell him that if he ever comes within ten feet of my fiancée again I'm going to hurt him real bad," he said, emphasizing the last four words.

Belinda smiled through the tears that were turning her eyes into pools of smoky quartz. "I told Raymond about you, and he says that exchanging Christmas cards will be the extent of our friendship. He didn't think he would be as understanding if you were my friend, and I was sleeping with him."

"I've changed my mind about Sunshine. I think I like him. And I'm sorry that I called him a chump and a con man."

Moving closer, Belinda kissed the cleft in his sexy chin. "You were jealous, when you had no need to be. It was you I was sleeping with, not Raymond."

"Lucky me. I'm the one who gets the nasty girl."

"You turned me into a nasty girl, Griffin Rice."

"Guilty as charged." Bending slightly, he swept her up in his arms. "Let's go inside and test the nasty meter again. But, before we do that we should talk about a few other things."

"What other things?"

"When do you want to get married? Do you want to live closer to Philly or here in Paoli? Do you want to increase our family—"

Belinda placed her hand over his mouth. "Stop talking, counselor. I can answer all those questions for you right now. I'd like to get married sometime this summer, preferably before the end of July. I'd prefer living in Paoli, but of course that means our daughters will have to change school districts. And yes, I'd like to begin increasing our family as soon as possible. Are there any other questions?"

He shook his head. "That's enough for now."

Griffin locked the door and carried Belinda up the staircase to what would become their bedroom. There was only the sound of measured breathing as she and the man holding her to his heart placed her on the bed. Leaning over, he brushed a kiss over her parted lips.

"Don't move. I know your birthday is a couple of days away, but I'd like to give you your gift now." Belinda leaned over on her elbows, her chin resting on her hands as she watched Griffin walk to the triple dresser and open a drawer.

He returned to the bed and sat down next to Belinda. Reaching for her left hand, he slipped the ring on her third finger, exhaling audibly. It was a perfect fit.

Belinda couldn't stop shaking. The brilliant emerald-cut diamond ring surrounded by baguette diamonds was magnificent. For the second time in a matter of minutes her eyes filled with tears. "I... I don't..."

"If you don't like it, then I'll take it back and you can pick out one that—"

"I love it, Griffin. I love you," she said, interrupting him. Putting her arms around his neck, she pressed her face to his warm throat. "When did you buy the ring?"

"I don't remember."

Belinda gave him a skeptical look. "I don't believe you."

"I bought it almost two weeks ago."

"You were that certain I'd marry you that you bought me a ring?"

"No. I bought it, hoping and praying that one day you'd accept it."

"Before you told me that you loved me?"

"I was going to do that—eventually."

"What am I going to do with you, Griffin Rice?"

Leaning back against the headboard, Griffin stared directly at Belinda. "You're going to marry me and give Sabrina and Layla a few brothers and sisters—technically they'll be cousins. And we'll grow more in love with each other as we grow old together."

"I'm never growing old, darling, and I don't want to stop being a nasty girl."

He trailed a series of kisses down the column of her neck, while unbuttoning her blouse. "Even when you're ninety-two and I'm ninety-seven you'll still be my beautiful, precious, nasty girl."

Belinda's breathing quickened as if she were panting, while Griffin stripped her of each article of clothing. She wanted him to go faster, but he seemed determined to take his time.

Her blouse, slacks and bra lay in a pool at the foot of the large bed. Once he'd taken off her panties, she lay completely naked and vulnerable to his ravenous gaze.

Going to her knees, she undressed her fiancé as slowly as he'd undressed her. And, when he lay on his back, all of his masculine magnificence was on display for her hungry gaze. A look of heated passion passed between them. This coming together would be different from all the others. The ring on her finger symbolized a shared commitment, a continuous bond of love that had no beginning or end. This night wasn't hers or Griffin's, but theirs.

Supporting herself with her hands, she lowered her body until her breasts were molded to his broad chest. "Do you want it nasty, or do you want it nice?"

Smiling, Griffin closed his eyes. "I'll take it any way and any how you choose to give it to me."

It was Belinda's turn to smile. "Like Tina Turner sang in 'Proud Mary,' I'm going to give it to you nice before it gets rough."

Griffin opened his eyes as an expression of unabashed carnal instinct spread across his face. "Serve it, Eaton." His rich, deep voice had dropped an octave. "Oh!" he bellowed within seconds of issuing the challenge when Belinda's mouth branded him her possession, swallowing back the expletive.

Her tongue took him to a place where he'd never been, and he surrendered all he was, had been and ever hoped to be. Her hot breath seared his loins and he went still, unable to protest or think of anything except the exquisite pleasure Belinda offered him. Clamping both hands over his mouth to muffle the groans crowding his throat, Griffin arched his pelvis off the bed. His passions were building quickly and he knew it was just a matter of time before he wouldn't be able to control where they'd be spent.

He sat up quickly, reaching for Belinda's hair. She emitted a small cry of surprise when he forced her to release his erection. Not giving her the opportunity to protest, he flipped her over and entered her in one, sure motion that buried his sex so deeply inside her that their bodies ceased to exist as separate entities.

Belinda's arms went around Griffin's waist as rivulets of sweat bathed his back and dotted her hands. She couldn't think of anything except the hard body atop hers as together they found a rhythm where they were in perfect harmony. The contractions began as flutters then increased in intensity until the hottest of fires swept over her, leaving tiny embers of ecstasy that lingered long after she'd returned from her free fall.

Reaching down, Griffin cupped her hips in his hands, lifting her higher and allowing for deeper penetration, then quickening his movements and bellowing out her name as he spilled his passion inside her hot, wet body. There was only the sound of their labored breathing in the stillness of the bedroom as they lay motionless, savoring the aftermath of a shared, sweet fulfillment.

As they lay in bed, their sexual passions momentarily sated, Belinda thought of her sister. She wished her sister could have been there to see her exchange vows with Griffin. But she knew Donna was smiling.

"Darling?"

Griffin smiled. "What is it, baby?"

"If we have a girl I want to name her Donna. But, if it's a boy then it'll be Grant."

Griffin felt a rush of tears behind his eyelids. He'd cried when told of his brother's death, and there was no doubt he would cry again—at the birth of his and Belinda's child. It didn't matter whether it was a boy or a girl. It would be loved, cherished and, of course, spoiled. He would make certain of that.

Turning his head, he fastened his mouth to the side of her neck. "Those are wonderful names."

Belinda smiled. "I didn't think you had it in you, but I think I'm going to give you a passing grade in the daddy category."

Griffin chuckled. "Does this mean I'm going to get an A?"

"Don't push it, Rice," she teased.

"What grade will you give me?"

She wrinkled her nose. "B-plus. If I give you an A then you'll end up with a swelled head."

"You keep cranking up that nasty meter and another head will remain swollen."

Belinda landed a soft punch on his shoulder. "You are so nasty, Griffin Rice."

Lifting his head, he flashed a wide grin. "I know, and you like it, don't you?"

"Hell, yeah!"

"That's my girl!" Griffin withdrew from Belinda and pulled her against his chest. "Did I tell you that I loved you?"

She wrinkled her nose again. "I don't remember. But you can tell me, just to refresh my memory."

And Griffin knew he would tell Belinda that he loved her—every day for the rest of their lives together.

Kappa Psi Kappa—these brothers are for real!

Award-winning author

ADRIANNE BYRD

Sinful Chocolate

Dark and delicious…

When a doctor gives playa extraordinaire Charlie six
months, he tries to make things right with all the
women he's wronged. Gisella Jacobs is busy launching
her new shop, Sinful Chocolate, when delectable
Charlie knocks at her door. But when she starts falling
for him, she finds it hard to heed her girlfriends'
warnings—and harder to resist him.

*Coming the first week of January 2009
wherever books are sold.*

KIMANI™
ROMANCE

www.kimanipress.com
www.myspace.com/kimanipress

KPAB0970109

Summer just got a little hotter!

National Bestselling Author

MELANIE SCHUSTER

A Case for *Romance*

With all her responsibilities, Ayanna Walker
hasn't had time for romance…until now. While
Johnny Phillips wants to share the future with
Ayanna, she's thinking only one thing: hot summer
fling! Can a man planning forever and a woman
planning the moment find the right time for love?

*Coming the first week of January 2009
wherever books are sold.*

KIMANI™
ROMANCE

www.kimanipress.com
www.myspace.com/kimanipress   KPMS0980109

The next sexy title in
The Black Stockings Society miniseries by

Favorite author

DARA GIRARD

Body
Chemistry

Every good girl deserves to be a little bit wicked....

New Black Stockings Society member Brenda Everton has
excelled in a man's world at the expense of her personal life.
Now, pairing sexy black stockings with a sexy new attitude,
she's meeting with her ex-husband, Dominic Ayers, to find
out whether passion can strike twice....

THE BLACK
STOCKINGS
SOCIETY

Four women. One club.
And a secret that will make
all their fantasies come true.

KIMANI™
ROMANCE

*Coming the first week
of January 2009
wherever books are sold.*

www.kimanipress.com
www.myspace.com/kimanipress   KPDG0990109

Award-winning authors

Victor McGlothin

Earl Sewell

Phillip Thomas Duck

whispers
betweenthesheets

**A scintillating anthology
filled with passion, drama and love.**

Join these three bestselling authors for
compelling stories in which three "playas"
learn some crucial lessons about love, lust…
and everything in between!

*Available the first week of January 2009
wherever books are sold.*

KIMANI PRESS™

www.kimanipress.com
www.myspace.com/kimanipress   KPWBTS0570109

New York Times Bestselling Author

BRENDA JACKSON

invites you to continue your journey
with the always sexy and always satisfying
Madaris family novels....

FIRE AND DESIRE
January 2009

SECRET LOVE
February 2009

TRUE LOVE
March 2009

SURRENDER
April 2009

ARABESQUE®

www.kimanipress.com
www.myspace.com/kimanipress

KPBJREISSUES09

REQUEST YOUR FREE BOOKS!

2 FREE NOVELS
PLUS 2 FREE GIFTS!

KIMANI ROMANCE ™

Love's ultimate destination!

YES! Please send me 2 FREE Kimani™ Romance novels and my 2 FREE gifts (gifts are worth about $10). After receiving them, if I don't wish to receive any more books, I can return the shipping statement marked "cancel." If I don't cancel, I will receive 4 brand-new novels every month and be billed just $4.69 per book in the U.S. or $5.24 per book in Canada, plus 25¢ shipping and handling per book and applicable taxes, if any*. That's a savings of over 20% off the cover price! I understand that accepting the 2 free books and gifts places me under no obligation to buy anything. I can always return a shipment and cancel at any time. Even if I never buy another book from Kimani Press, the two free books and gifts are mine to keep forever.

168 XDN EF2D   368 XDN EF3T

Name	(PLEASE PRINT)	
Address		Apt. #
City	State/Prov.	Zip/Postal Code

Signature (if under 18, a parent or guardian must sign)

Mail to The Reader Service:
IN U.S.A.: P.O. Box 1867, Buffalo, NY 14240-1867
IN CANADA: P.O. Box 609, Fort Erie, Ontario L2A 5X3

Not valid to current subscribers of Kimani Romance books.

Want to try two free books from another line?
Call 1-800-873-8635 or visit www.morefreebooks.com.

* Terms and prices subject to change without notice. N.Y. residents add applicable sales tax. Canadian residents will be charged applicable provincial taxes and GST. Offer not valid in Quebec. This offer is limited to one order per household. All orders subject to approval. Credit or debit balances in a customer's account(s) may be offset by any other outstanding balance owed by or to the customer. Please allow 4 to 6 weeks for delivery. Offer available while quantities last.

Your Privacy: Kimani Press is committed to protecting your privacy. Our Privacy Policy is available online at www.eHarlequin.com or upon request from the Reader Service. From time to time we make our lists of customers available to reputable third parties who may have a product or service of interest to you. If you would prefer we not share your name and address, please check here. ☐

KROM08R

**These women are about to discover that every passion
has a price…and some secrets are impossible to keep.**

NATIONAL BESTSELLING AUTHOR

ROCHELLE ALERS

After Hours

A deliciously scandalous novel that brings together
three very different women, united by the secret lives
they lead. Adina, Sybil and Karla all lead seemingly
charmed, luxurious lives, yet each also harbors a
surprising secret that is about to spin out of control.

"Alers paints such vivid descriptions that when Jolene
becomes the target of a murderer, you almost feel
as though someone you know is in great danger."
—*Library Journal* on *No Compromise*

***Coming the first week of March
wherever books are sold.***

sepia™

www.kimanipress.com   KPRA1220308

NATIONAL BESTSELLING AUTHOR

ROCHELLE ALERS

invites you to meet the Whitfields of New York....

Tessa, Faith and Simone Whitfield know all about coordinating
other people's weddings, and not so much about arranging
their own love lives. But in the space of one unforgettable year,
all three will meet intriguing men who just might bring them their
very own happily ever after....

Long Time Coming
June 2008

The Sweetest Temptation
July 2008

Taken by Storm
August 2008

ARABESQUE®

www.kimanipress.com

KPALERSTRIL08